For more than forty years,
Yearling has been the leading name
in classic and award-winning literature
for young readers.

Yearling books feature children's
favorite authors and characters,
providing dynamic stories of adventure,
humor, history, mystery, and fantasy.

Trust Yearling paperbacks to entertain,
inspire, and promote the love of reading
in all children.

**READ ALL THE BOOKS IN
THE CAPED 6TH GRADER SERIES**

Happy Birthday, Hero!

Totally Toxic

Lightning Strikes!

4

Cabin Fever

Zoe Quinn

ILLUSTRATED BY BRIE SPANGLER

A YEARLING BOOK

TO SHANNON, MY OWN SUPERHERO

WITH SPECIAL THANKS TO
LISA FIEDLER

Published by Yearling, an imprint of Random House Children's Books
a division of Random House, Inc., New York

Visit us on the Web! www.randomhouse.com/kids

Educators and librarians, for a variety of teaching tools, visit us at
www.randomhouse.com/teachers

Library of Congress Cataloging-in-Publication Data
is available upoon request.

ISBN: 978-0-440-42082-8 (tr. pbk.)
ISBN: 978-0-385-90307-3 (lib. bdg.)

Printed in the United States of America

February 2007

10 9 8 7 6 5 4 3 2 1

ONE of the best things about being a kid—superpowered or otherwise—is going to camp. It seems like there's a camp for everything: band camp, dance camp, hockey camp, science camp, baseball camp, fencing camp, art camp . . . and of course, there's *my* camp. . . .

"Throw me those shin guards, will ya?"

I was sitting on the floor in my best friend Emily's room, watching her toss shorts and T-shirts into her very chic designer duffel bag. Emily was heading off to soccer camp the next morning. Last year, I'd gone with her. This year . . . well, I had different plans.

"Oh, and the goalie jersey, please."

I grabbed the guards. "Here you go," I said, lobbing them toward the bed. Then I pulled the jersey out of a dresser drawer and tossed that to Emily. She tucked it into the bag, then stuffed her blow-dryer and a handful of hair accessories into the side pocket.

"I can't believe you're not coming with me," she said, dropping onto the bed with a sigh. "And all because the camp lost your paperwork."

I gave her a sad shrug. The paperwork thing wasn't exactly true (which I hated).

My mom had filled out the forms and written the check and given the envelope to me to mail—which I hadn't done. Not because I'm irresponsible, but because Grandpa had already told me I was going to a different camp. I was going to Camp Courageous, a special camp for superheroes.

Three weeks later, Mom called the soccer camp to ask about my cabin assignment, and that's when the director explained that they'd never received my paperwork, and that he was sorry but it was too late, the camp was full.

"It's such a bummer," Emily was saying. "I'm going to miss you."

"I'll miss you, too," I said. "But we can write to each other."

"I guess," said Emily. "That reminds me. Did you bring your camp address?"

"Uh-huh," I said, reaching into my pocket and pulling out a slip of paper. I handed it to Emily.

She read the address and smiled. "Camp Courageous? You're going to a place called Camp Courageous?"

I felt a tingle of pride. "Yep. Isn't that a cool name?"

"Sure," she said, putting the address carefully into her duffel. "But *courageous* kinda makes me wonder about the sort of activities they're going to have there."

"Makes me wonder, too," I said, biting back the excitement in my voice.

The truth was, I couldn't wait to find out.

WELCOME to CAMP COURAGEOUS

The premier camp for up-and-coming superheroes! Nestled in a quaint, woodsy setting on the sandy shores of pristine Lake Victory, Camp Courageous provides young superheroes with the opportunity to improve their superskills while learning to work with other heroes. The weeklong experience includes teamwork training, individual power development, disaster-control education, and arts and crafts.

"Zoe," said Mom, coming into my room later that day, "I've been thinking . . ."

I quickly tucked the brochure I was reading for the hundredth time into my suitcase. "Yes?"

"Do you think the twelve pairs of underwear we packed will be enough?"

I rolled my eyes. "Mom, I'm only going away for a week!"

"Well, I just think it's good to be prepared," she said as she walked across the room toward my dresser. "What if you fall in the lake with your clothes on and have to change? That'll call for an extra pair, won't it? Or what if your suitcase gets infested with ants and they make a nest in that pretty pair of pink and yellow polka-dot underpants?"

I gave my mother a sidelong look. "Ants in my underpants? Mom, are you trying to talk me out of going to camp?"

Mom gave me a tiny smile. "Maybe." She dug into a drawer and pulled out a handful of underwear, then came over to where my suitcase was open on the bed and dropped them in. "Just to be safe," she said.

I laughed. "Whatever."

"It's just that . . . well, it was bad enough last summer, sending you off to soccer camp, and that was only for three nights. This time, you're going to be gone a whole week!"

I stood up and gave her a hug. "Don't worry, Mom. I'll be fine."

"I know you will," she said, sighing. "It makes me feel better to know that Grandpa Zack went there when he was your age. And he knows the camp director, which is a lucky thing, or we'd never have been able to get you in at such a late date."

"Uh, yeah. Right. Very lucky." I turned away, feeling a little guilty about the whole paperwork scam.

4

"What's this?" said Mom, reaching into my suitcase.

My heart skipped a beat when she pulled out the brochure. "Oh . . . uh . . ."

"I didn't realize Grandpa Zack had given you a brochure about the camp."

"I, uh, I guess I forgot to show it to you."

Mom opened the folded pamphlet, revealing the colorful photos of the cabins, the campfire pit, the lake with its fleet of canoes and paddleboats, kids riding horses, and a pretty counselor teaching a basket-weaving class. Mom began to read.

I panicked. If she read the part about developing powers, the secret would be out.

"Oh, they have archery," she said. "That sounds exciting. And arts and crafts. Maybe you can make me a macramé plant holder."

I leaned over and looked at the brochure.

WELCOME to CAMP COURAGEOUS

The premier camp for eleven- to fourteen-year-olds! Nestled in a quaint, woodsy setting on the sandy shores of pristine Lake Victory, Camp Courageous provides young campers with the opportunity to improve their social skills while learning to work with other children. The weeklong experience includes swimming, tennis, archery, horseback riding, and arts and crafts.

Huh? It was the same brochure I'd just read, but the words had changed. Instead of *superheroes,* it said *campers,* and instead of *disaster-control education . . . archery?*

Mom handed me the brochure and went back to the dresser to get an armful of extra socks. I looked at the brochure—before my eyes, all the words went back to the way they'd been. I read on.

A Word About the Courageous Cup

The most important and memorable element of your stay at our camp will be the Courageous Cup competition. It is an exciting three-day contest that challenges campers in a most surprising way.

A car horn sounded in the driveway.

"That's Grandpa," I said, closing the suitcase before Mom could pack any more unmentionables. I snatched it up, grabbed my superbackpack, then hurried out of the room and down the stairs with Mom on my heels. My dad was waiting in the front hall, dressed for work.

"Have a good time, kiddo," he said, giving my ponytail a tug. "Remember . . . don't get too close to the campfire, always swim with a buddy, and if the cafeteria serves something called mystery meat, don't eat it."

"Got it, Dad."

"Maybe I should cancel my Save the Whales meeting and ride to camp with you," said Mom, wringing her hands.

"Don't do that," I said. "Really. Those whales need you."

She smiled, but her eyes were shiny with tears. "Be careful up there in the wilderness," she said, only half joking.

"I will. See you in a week."

Outside, I tossed my suitcase into the backseat of the blue convertible and jumped in beside it. From the driver's seat, Gran tooted the horn to my parents, who were waving from the front porch, then took off. Looking at me in the rearview mirror, she grinned.

"How many?" she asked knowingly.

"Twelve pairs!" I said. "Then she threw in an extra bunch." I explained Mom's ant theory and Gran laughed out loud.

Grandpa chuckled, too. "Only your mother would worry about bugs taking up residence in a pair of bloomers."

"Poor Maria," said Gran. "She gets so nervous when it comes to you, Zoe. If she only knew that you were going to be surrounded by superheroes, the protectors of the universe."

"Tell me more about Camp Courageous, Grandpa," I said, settling into the soft white leather of the backseat.

"Well, for one thing, they have great arts and crafts."

"Tell her about the Courageous Cup competition," Gran prompted.

I could see Grandpa Zack blushing.

"Yeah, tell me," I said. "I just read something about it in the brochure. Sounds like a big deal."

"It's the most hallowed tradition at Camp Courageous, a competition to test the campers on what they've learned during their stay. Everyone takes part. The counselors pair up cabins— one boys' cabin with one girls' cabin—into teams. Then the teams are given difficult tasks to accomplish. Whichever team performs the most tasks successfully wins. It's a great honor to be on the winning team."

"So if everyone takes part, that means you were in the Courageous Cup competition when you went to camp," I said.

"Yes," said Grandpa, "I was in it."

"Don't be so modest, Zack," said Gran, flicking the turn signal and steering the car onto a narrow dirt road that led into the woods. "Zoe, your grandfather's team won the cup! His name and the names of his teammates are engraved on a giant trophy in the display case in the main lodge."

"Grandpa, that's so cool!"

"I was twelve years old, just like you, Zoe. The name of my cabin was Valiant, and I had three great cabinmates. Terrific lads. We'd become good friends over the week, and then it was time to prove ourselves in the cup competition, which consists of three separate challenges."

I laughed. "Challenges? Unless they bring in supervillains for the campers to defeat, I can't imagine anything would be too challenging to a bunch of superkids."

"You're absolutely right. Which is why the main rule of the Courageous Cup contest is that you *can't* use your superpowers."

I almost slid off the seat in surprise. "Huh? I don't get it."

"The beginning of camp week is about training," Grandpa explained. "Learning, growing as a superhero, using your powers and improving them."

"Okay..."

"But even the most powerful heroes in the universe can't succeed unless they understand the meaning of teamwork. Cooperation. That's what the cup contest is all about. When you don't have your superpowers and gadgets at your disposal, you have to rely on teamwork. It's a good lesson for heroes. You'd be surprised at how difficult it is for some of them to put aside their egos and let others lend a hand."

Gran had turned off the highway and we were driving along

rural back roads. The scenery was lush and green and the air was fresh and clean. Finally, Gran turned the car into the gravel parking lot of Camp Courageous.

A man with bushy white hair came rushing over to the car. "Zip, is that you?" he cried.

"Sure is," said Grandpa. "Zoe, this is a member of the Superhero Federation board of directors. In the summer, he runs Camp Courageous. We used to call him Battlin' Bertram."

Before I could say nice to meet you, the director flung open the car door and tugged Grandpa out. "Zip, you old rascal, it's great to see you!" He threw his arms around my grandfather and hugged him; then Battlin' Bertram proceeded to lift Zip right over his head . . . with one hand!

Grandpa laughed. "Well, I see someone's kept up his training!"

"I have to, Zip, old boy, if I'm going to handle these young ones!" He put Grandpa down, then went around to open the car door for Gran.

"Sally, my dear."

"Nice to see you, Bert. How's Matilda?"

"She's just fine. Running the mess hall these days. She feels it's her sworn duty to make sure these growing heroes get their proper nutrition."

"Hope she's done away with the mystery meat selection," Grandpa grumbled through a grin.

"That was her first order of business!" Bertram chuckled.

Grandpa reached into the backseat and got my suitcase while I climbed out with my backpack. "This is Zoe," he said. "Also known as Kid Zoom. She takes after me."

"Ah, so I have another speed demon on my hands this year." Bert shook my hand. "Hello there, Zoe."

"Nice to meet you, sir."

"Bertram was one of my teammates the year we won the Courageous Cup," Grandpa added.

"That's right," said Bertram. "Make sure you check out the trophy in the display case, Zoe. Maybe your name will appear on it one day, too! Well, I need to head over to the archery field and make sure the targets have been properly laser-proofed. We've got a kid in from New Zealand this summer . . . shoots laser beams out of his elbows. Great to see you, Zack, Sally."

Grandpa shook Bertram's hand, and the director walked away.

"I guess I should get going," I said, glancing across the parking lot; through the trees and cabins, I caught a glimpse of Lake Victory glistening in the sunshine.

"You have a good time, dear," said Gran, kissing me on the cheek.

Grandpa gave my shoulder a squeeze. "I know you'll make me proud," he said.

They hopped back into the little blue car; Gran honked the horn, then peeled out in a spray of gravel. As I watched them drive off, I got a funny feeling in the pit of my stomach, as if there were a rock sitting there. It was beginning to dawn on me that I was going to be away from home for a whole week, at a camp where I didn't know a single supersoul. I guess being super doesn't mean you never feel lonely or homesick.

Clutching my suitcase and backpack, I headed in the direction of the cabins.

CHAPTER

2

SCHEDULE

SATURDAY, Day 1—
Campers Arrive
Cabin Assignments
6:00 p.m. Dinner
Campfire Sing-along

THE place was crawling with kids. Superkids, that is. Of course, you'd never guess if you didn't know. It really did look just like a regular bunch of campers, decked out in cargo shorts and Camp Courageous T-shirts; some were already in their swimsuits, making their way toward the lake, while others wore sneakers and crisp white shorts and polos, heading for the tennis courts.

I stood nervously in what looked like the center of camp, beside the flagpole, wondering where to go next.

"Hi there," said a tall, red-haired girl in a STAFF T-shirt. She was wearing a whistle around her neck. Her stick-on name tag said her name was Amanda.

"Looking for your cabin?" she asked.

I nodded.

"Name?"

"Richards. Zoe Richards. Uh, Kid Zoom, if that helps."

Amanda consulted her clipboard and smiled. "Kid Zoom. You're in cabin Intrepid, which means I'm your counselor."

"Great."

Amanda laughed. "We'll see if you think so when training begins."

I couldn't tell if she was kidding or not. "So, which way to Intrepid?" I asked.

"C'mon." Amanda put a hand on my shoulder. "I'll walk you there."

We wound our way down the path to a sturdy-looking little wood cabin. Amanda held the screen door open and I stepped inside to see three girls in various stages of unpacking.

"Hi," I said, putting my suitcase down.

"Girls, this is Zoe," said Amanda. "Zoe, this is Melanie, Casey, and Megan."

We exchanged hellos, and one of the girls—Megan—pointed out which bunk was mine. She was tiny and looked as though she had energy to burn. Her light brown hair was wound into two thick braids and she had dimples in her cheeks.

"When you're done unpacking, Intrepids, come find me by the lake," said Amanda, making her exit. "We can start planning our strategy for the Courageous Cup."

Wow, I thought. *This competition must be really important!* I'd been expecting some icebreaker games or at least a tour of camp or something to start with. For the first time, I began to wonder if I was cup competition material.

A friendly voice interrupted my thoughts. "So, do you have a Super name?"

I turned to Megan, who'd asked the question. "Kid Zoom," I said. "How about you?"

"I'm still working on it," she said. "My cousin Mighty Mike, who's my supercoach back home, likes Air Meg, because I'm a flyer. But I'm sorta leaning toward Mega-Megan."

"Mega-Megan is a great Super name," I said.

"Yeah, I think it has a nice ring to it." Megan tossed a pair of pajamas on one of the lower bunks. "Hope you don't mind the top bunk, Zoe. See, since I'm a flyer, I sometimes accidentally levitate in my sleep. Having the top bunk to hold me down will keep me from floating around the room."

"Top bunk's fine," I said. "So you can really fly? That's awesome."

Megan nodded.

"My uncle Al is a flyer," Casey chimed in. Her blond hair fell in soft curls to her shoulders and her eyes were dark brown and friendly. "Maybe you've heard of him? His Super name is Altitude. Anyway, he took me flying once, kind of like a piggy-back ride, only in the sky." She paused, holding back a grin. "I threw up in his hair."

"Ewww." Megan laughed. "Poor Uncle Al."

"Gross," I agreed.

"Yeah, it was pretty icky," Casey admitted.

"I'd probably do the same thing," said Melanie. "I get a little queasy just jumping over tall buildings."

"I love jumping over tall buildings," Megan said. "How about you, Zoe?"

"I haven't tried jumping a building yet, but just a few weeks ago I had to leap into a really big tree. It was fun, actually, except the tiger made it a little scary."

"Tiger?" said Melanie, her crystal blue eyes growing wide.

I gave a little wave. "Long story."

I opened my suitcase and began to unpack. The first thing I took out was the pink and green bikini Emily had helped me pick out at the mall.

"Ooooh, cute swimsuit," said Casey. "I forgot to pack my bikini. I only brought a one-piece." She held up a shimmery blue bathing suit.

"Great color," I said. "And I like the way the straps cross in back."

"Thanks. I like it because it's glittery. And it's also indestructible."

"Cool," said Melanie. She was the tallest of the four of us. Her straight brown hair reached all the way to her waist. "By the way, did anybody notice that really cute counselor? The blond one with the shaggy haircut. He's a total hottie."

"That's Simon," Casey said. "I checked out his name tag. And when he told me how to find the cabin, he had an English accent."

"I love English accents," said Megan in a dreamy voice.

"Me too," said Melanie; she was removing a superhot pair of sunglasses from her duffel bag and placing them on the dresser closest to her bed.

"I like your shades," I said.

"They're okay," said Melanie. "I mean, I'm not really into wearing sunglasses, but I don't have a choice. Sometimes I accidentally melt things with my eyes."

I raised my eyebrows. "Oh. Yikes."

"Yeah. These were made by the tech guys at the Federation."

She giggled. "But my mom thinks I bought them at the mall with my birthday money."

"What's your power?" Megan asked me.

"Well, I have superstrength, but I'm finding out that that's pretty common. And I can shoot laser beams from my eyes, though I've only done that a couple of times, and never by accident! My real specialty is speed."

"Ah . . . so you're fast."

I smiled. "Superfast."

"Good," said Casey. "Then you'll be the one we send ahead to get us a good seat at the campfire."

I grinned, already feeling much less lonely.

"How about you?" Melanie asked Casey. "What's your specialty?"

"Superhearing. I can hear a mouse sneeze from like, twelve miles away."

"Doesn't that make it hard to sleep?" I asked, silently hoping, for Casey's sake, that none of us snored.

"Nah. I've gotten pretty good at turning it on and off. So it's not usually a problem."

I started unpacking; since the other girls had had a head start, they were nearly finished.

"Why don't you use your superspeed?" Melanie suggested. "You'll be unpacked in no time."

I felt a flutter of nerves. This would be the first time my new cabinmates would see my powers in action. What if I couldn't make them work? Or what if I started going so fast I tripped, or burned a hole in the floor, or started flinging clothes around the room uncontrollably? That had happened once at home, back when I had just found about my powers, and it had taken ages

16

to clean up! But I guessed that was what I there for—to get good at using my powers.

"Um . . . okay." I began pulling clothes out of my suitcase at warp speed, dashing back and forth from the dresser. It was kind of strange to be able to use my power in front of other kids and not have to worry about it. Actually, it was very liberating.

"Zoe, that is so cool," said Megan. "You're, like, a blur."

"If I could move like that," said Casey, "I'd never be late for school again."

Minutes later, we were on our way to the lake.

We found Amanda waiting for us, pacing up and down on the shore.

"Okay, Intrepids," she said, clapping her hands and flashing a big, confident smile. "Let's get down to business!"

I looked out over the beautiful blue lake. Campers were splashing in the shallow water; farther out, some boys were having a diving contest off a raft. Kids were racing paddleboats and wobbling in canoes. I found myself wishing we'd thought to change into our bathing suits. Maybe we could have gotten "down to business" while splashing and diving and racing.

Amanda gave a sharp blast on her whistle. "When I came to Camp Courageous as a new superhero," she began, "I had one goal and one goal only: to win the Courageous Cup! So, for one solid week, my cabinmates and I trained as hard as we could . . . and we did it. We won! You should know, it's not always easy, and sometimes it gets downright dangerous. You're Supers, after all, so we hold you to very high standards. Now, Intrepids, it's your turn. I can tell just by looking at you that you girls have what it takes to win! And from the looks of the boys' cabin you've been teamed with . . ."

"Boys' cabin?" Melanie smiled at Amanda and her eyes lit up. No . . . I mean they literally *lit up*. Her pale blue irises seemed to become blue flames, glowing with heat. "I like the sound of that." Her dreamy gaze had fallen on the metal whistle in Amanda's hand, and I watched in amazement as the whistle began to turn a blazing red!

Amanda dropped the whistle, shaking her burned fingers. "Ouch!"

"Sorry!" cried Melanie.

"No problem," said Amanda. "You can't fight what comes naturally."

I grinned. "Maybe you should keep your sunglasses handy when we meet those boys," I suggested.

"What's your power, Amanda?" Casey asked.

"Supervision," Amanda said. "I can see for miles, so if you're thinking about slacking off during practice, forget it." She laughed, then went on talking about teamwork, tradition, and the thrill of victory. I tried to stay focused, but my attention kept drifting to my fellow campers, having fun in the lake.

The afternoon sun was low in the sky by the time Amanda finished with her pep talk. "So . . . are you girls ready to work?"

"Yes, ma'am."

"Sure thing."

"Absolutely."

"Definitely!"

A loud clanging sounded in the distance.

"That's the dinner bell," said Amanda. "Go on up to the mess hall. I'll meet you there once I've dropped my stuff off." Scanning her clipboard, she walked away.

"I think the mess hall is over that hill," said Megan.

18

We started up the steep path. When we reached the crest, we could see the large main lodge, which housed the dining room. The wide windows were glowing warm in the dusky light, and I could smell the rich aromas of saucy baked beans and tangy macaroni and cheese.

Suddenly, I realized I was starving.

Apparently, my bunkmates were, too. As if we could read each other's minds (which we couldn't—at least, not as far as I knew!), we all began to run at once. For kicks, I turned on my superspeed. I could hear them laughing as I left them behind.

My plan was get into the mess hall first and save us a good table, and I was heading for the entrance at a good clip when something caught my eye.

It was Bertram, the camp director, with Simon, the shaggy-haired hottie. I did a double take, then dug my sneakers into the stony path and came skidding to a halt.

I wasn't stopping to admire the cute counselor. I was stopping because Bertram and the cute counselor were deep in conversation with someone I knew.

That someone was Gil Hunt, Howie's grandfather.

And standing nearby, looking completely confused, was Howie.

CHAPTER 3

THERE had to be some sort of mistake. Howie Hunt . . . at superhero camp?

No way! No . . . *way*!

Howie was standing a few yards away from his grandfather and Simon, ignoring their whispered conversation as his eyes scanned the campgrounds. He looked curious but also sort of disappointed. There was a duffel bag at his feet.

I was still standing there staring at Howie when my bunk-mates caught up to me.

"Something wrong?" Megan asked.

"Very wrong," I said. "See that kid over there? He's a friend of mine from home. He lives next door to me."

Casey looked over at Howie. "Wow, that's so cool that you have someone from home who's a Super like you. None of the kids in my neighborhood are super."

"That's just it," I said. "Howie isn't super. I can't imagine how he even heard about Camp Courageous."

"I wouldn't worry about it," said Melanie. "If he's not super, then he won't be on the official camp roster. And if he's not on the roster, Bertram will tell him he can't stay and send him home. It must just be some mix-up."

But I was surprised to see Bertram throw up his hands, turn on his heel, and walk away. As he came closer to where we were standing, he called over his shoulder, "There's just no reasoning with you, Gil. Simon, you handle this. Whatever you decide is fine with me!"

When Bertram disappeared around the bend, Mr. Hunt went back to his conversation with Simon. Howie's grandfather looked very upset, gesturing urgently with his arms as he spoke to the counselor. By now, Howie had wandered a few feet away and was examining the bark of a tall pine tree.

"Who's that man talking to Simon?" Melanie asked.

"Howie's grandpa," I said, watching as Mr. Hunt stamped his foot and shook his finger at Simon. "It doesn't look like he's going to take no for an answer." I frowned. "I wish I could hear what they were talking about."

"I can," said Casey.

"That's right . . . you *can*!" I turned to her with a desperate look. "Oh, Casey. Would you mind? It doesn't make any sense that Howie's here!"

"Well, I try not to listen in on private conversations unless someone is in danger, but since you're friends with this Howie kid, I guess it'll be okay."

"Mel and I will go in and save you guys some seats," said

Megan, "and we'll grab you some mac and cheese before they run out."

"Yeah," said Melanie. "You two stay out here and eavesdrop—superstyle!"

They continued toward the lodge. Casey pushed a curly lock of blond hair behind her right ear and tilted her head in the direction of Howie's grandpa and Simon.

I held my breath while Casey listened.

Mr. Hunt continued to stamp and gesture, and Simon nodded, looking patient and understanding. Finally, they shook hands. Mr. Hunt called Howie back over and said something to him, then patted him on the head and walked off toward the parking lot. Howie stared after his grandfather until Simon gave him a friendly nudge and led him up the path to the cabins.

"What did they say?" I asked eagerly.

Casey looked a little confused. "I thought you said that Howie kid wasn't super."

"He's not," I said.

"He is," said Casey.

My mouth dropped open.

"At least, he *will* be. According to his grandpa," Casey said. "He told Simon that Howie's powers haven't shown themselves yet, probably because he doesn't turn twelve till next month. But he's sure that being here at camp will bring them on. He said he was a full-fledged superhero back in the day, and that means it's almost a lock that Howie will be super, too. Simon started to tell him that there are no genetic guarantees, but the old guy would have none of it. He told Simon that as a member of the Camp Courageous Alumni Association, he had every right to enroll Howie."

I felt a little dizzy. Gil Hunt . . . Grandpa Zack's business's next-door neighbor . . . Sweetbriar's premier florist (at least, according to him) . . . a *superhero*? And *Howie*? It was just too unbelievable.

But now that I thought about it, there had always been some things about Mr. Hunt I'd never understood. For as long as I could remember, he and Grandpa had seemed sort of competitive. And Gil made Howie train over and over for the Little League team when everyone knew there wasn't a hope of Howie's being picked; Howie wasn't totally useless, he just seemed to have some sort of repelling-magnet thing going on where catching balls was concerned. I also remembered how Mr. Hunt had been so anxious to have Howie work with the police during our school internship project—it must have been because he expected Howie to become a superhero one day and he thought that would be good practice!

"One more thing . . . ," Casey went on. "I definitely got the feeling that your pal Howie has no idea what's going on. From what Simon was saying, Howie has no idea that this is a camp for superkids or even that he is . . . well, might be . . . a superkid himself."

"His grandfather didn't tell him before he brought him here?" I asked in disbelief. "Poor Howie. He's gonna be totally freaked out when he sees kids flying and melting things and who knows what else."

Casey looked sympathetic. "I think you should be the one to break it to him, Zoe. The sooner the better, too."

She was right, of course. I'd have to tell him. I had no idea if that would be breaking the Superhero Federation rules, but I knew in my heart that Howie needed to know the truth.

23

"I'll tell him right after dinner," I said.

The only question was . . . how?

By the time Simon brought Howie in to dinner, my friends and I were starting on dessert. Simon led Howie to a table of boys who I guessed were his bunkmates. They seemed welcoming enough; I just hoped nobody used any superpowers until I had a chance to talk to Howie and explain. I was so busy watching Howie—and making sure he didn't see me—that I didn't even enjoy my chocolate pudding.

After dinner, I tramped around camp looking for Howie. Kids were hurrying from cabin to cabin, meeting up with friends before going to the campfire. Finally, I spotted Howie sitting on the front steps of the Bravery cabin, leaning against the wooden railing. As I made my way through the trees, I saw his bunkmates come out of the cabin and join him on the little porch.

"Ready for the campfire, Howie?" asked one. He had dark hair, and even from the trees I could see that his eyes were a dark chocolate brown. He looked like a football star or one of those hunky guys you'd see on a wall-sized poster in an expensive clothing store. He offered his invitation with a big smile, but Howie just shook his head.

"C'mon," urged his second cabinmate, a red-haired boy, pulling on a sweatshirt. "It'll be fun. I saw some cute girls at registration. Maybe we can meet some of them."

"No thanks," said Howie. "You guys go ahead."

"Okay," said the third kid, who was lanky and wore his light hair in a buzz cut. "Want us to bring you back some s'mores?"

24

"No, thank you," Howie said politely. "I'm allergic to marshmallows."

The three boys looked at one another; they seemed to understand that Howie needed to be left alone for the moment. They probably thought he was homesick.

When they were gone, I approached the porch.

"Hi."

Howie looked up and his eyes went round. "Zoe?"

"Yep, it's me. Surprise."

"What are you doing here?"

"Same as you. Going to camp."

"This isn't the camp I signed up for," he said glumly. "I wanted to go to science camp."

"Science camp, huh?" I couldn't help grinning; Howie was about to find out that he was in for the experiment of a lifetime!

"This morning, I was all set to go to the best science camp in the county when Grandpa Gil stormed in and told us there had been a terrible accident. One of the counselors-in-training had forgotten to turn off a Bunsen burner and the entire place burned to the ground. No one got hurt, but the camp had to be closed down for rebuilding. Then he said not to worry, because he had found me a better camp. A supercamp."

I cocked an eyebrow. "He told you it was a supercamp?"

Howie nodded.

"Oh." I wrinkled my nose. "So . . . you know, then?"

"Know what?"

"Know that Camp Courageous is, well . . . *super.*"

Howie looked around. "That's what Grandpa Gil said. But I don't see what's so super about it. I mean, it's all right, I guess. Trees, cabins, canoes—typical camp stuff. Nice enough, if you're into that kind of thing. But I don't think I'd call it super."

Now I understood. When Mr. Hunt said the camp was super, Howie just thought he meant it was great or terrific.

"Uh . . . Howie . . . ," I began. "I have something to tell you. And you might find it very hard to believe, but I promise you, it is absolutely, completely, and totally true." I took a deep breath. "The good news is that the science camp didn't burn down."

"What? I mean, that's good. But why would my grandpa—"

"This camp isn't a regular camp," I said, interrupting him. "Not at all. It's special. Very special. For very special kids. And by special, I mean . . . super." I swallowed hard, trying to think of how to say what I needed to tell him. "And by super, I mean . . . well, I mean . . ."

He looked at me, waiting.

I leaned down, grasped the corner of the porch step with one hand, and lifted the entire Bravery cabin off the ground.

Howie shrieked, grasping the railing and holding on for dear life.

Gently, I lowered the cabin back to the ground.

"That's what I mean by super," I said. But Howie didn't hear me.

He'd fainted.

CHAPTER 4

I sat down on the porch step and waited for Howie to come to. Resting my chin in my hand, I watched the fireflies twinkle in the darkness, listened to my fellow campers singing silly songs in the distance, and thought about the gooey, sweet s'mores I was missing out on. I probably could have run down to the fire at superspeed, grabbed a s'more or two, and been back before Howie woke up, but I couldn't just leave him. It would be very unsuperhero-like of me, not to mention plain inconsiderate.

After a minute or two, I heard him groan. "Where am I?" he asked, blinking.

I decided to give it to him straight. "You're at Camp Courageous," I told him. "It's a camp for kids with superpowers. I have superpowers. My bunkmates have superpowers. *Your* bunkmates have superpowers. The counselors have superpowers, and, if your grandpa's theory is correct, by the time this week is over, you'll have superpowers, too. That is, if you can manage not to faint every time somebody does something super. See, it's all about the super, Howie. Me, you, everyone else . . . super, super, super. Got it? Good. Now, let's go on down to that campfire pit and melt us some marshmallows, shall we?"

Howie looked at me as if I were crazy. I'd expected as much. I sighed.

"I know it sounds nuts, but it's a fact. I was pretty amazed when I first found out, but I got used to it. And you'll get used to it, too."

I knew I wasn't doing a terrific job of explaining to Howie. It was just such a huge, crazy concept. It occurred to me that this was the first time I'd had to put it into words for someone—and it would probably be the last, since telling Ordinaries about superpowers was forbidden.

A cool breeze rippled through the trees. The stars winked in the velvety sky. Howie's eyes were locked on mine for what seemed like forever. And just when I thought he would never say another word to me in his life, he said, "Okay, Zoe."

It was my turn to blink. "'Okay, Zoe'? That's all you have to say? 'Okay'?"

Howie shrugged. "Well, here's the thing. You've been my friend for my whole life, and in all that time, you've never lied to me, so I have no reason to think you're lying to me now. Plus, I saw you pick up this cabin with one hand. If I were to apply logic to this situation, I would have to say that the data you just presented provides conclusive proof of what you're saying. So I believe you. I believe this camp is for superkids, and that you're super, and that maybe I'll be super, too. And I believe you when you say I'll get used to it. I may not understand it, but I definitely believe it."

"Oh. Well, all right, then." I shrugged. "I think for the moment, though, you probably shouldn't let on that you don't have your powers yet. Just to keep things from getting any more complicated than they already are. I know that Ordinaries aren't supposed to know about Supers, but I have no idea if there are any rules about Supers knowing about non-Supers—even temporary ones—being among them!"

"I guess that's good advice," he agreed. "I can live with that—but what I really want to know is why on earth anyone thinks *I* have superpowers?"

"You inherited them," I said. "At least, that's the theory. It's hard to tell who's going to get them and who isn't. The gene is pretty unpredictable." I felt the need to add, "Right now, let's just hope you've got it and it's taking its time coming to the surface."

"Well, if I have inherited it, who did I inherit it from?"

"From your grandpa Gil."

For a second, I thought he might faint again. His face was totally blank. Then he burst out laughing. "My grandpa Gil is a superhero?"

"A retired one, just like my grandpa Zack."

"Wow." He let the idea sink in for a minute. "I mean, of all people . . . Although it does explain a lot. He's always asking me to lift heavy things for him, and pointing out road signs that are really far away and asking if I can read them. I guess that makes sense now." Howie took a deep breath and let it out. "Wow," he repeated.

I remembered the day Grandpa Zack broke the news to me about my powers. I knew exactly how Howie felt, but there was so much I still had to tell him.

"How about this . . . ," I said. "Tomorrow, during free time, you and I can go out for a canoe ride around the lake and I'll explain everything to you."

"Okay," he said. "That sounds good."

From the campfire pit, we could hear the other campers laughing and singing:

> *"We are the superkids who come to Camp Courageous.*
> *The counselors are awesome and the campers are outrageous . . . ."*

"So, Howie, how about getting some of those s'mores?"

"I'm allergic to marshmallows," he reminded me, but he stood up anyway and followed me down the path.

"Right," I said.

"Do you think that will be a major problem?" he said anxiously.

"Not knowing your grandpa Gil was a superhero?"

"No. Being allergic to marshmallows. I mean, s'mores are an essential part of camp, right?" There was a yelp and a muffled thud as he tripped over a rock and almost face-planted. "Ouch!"

I helped him up, thinking that marshmallows were going to be the least of his problems for the upcoming week.

✧

The Intrepids awoke the next morning to the sound of a whistle blaring. I sat bolt upright in my bunk and nearly clunked my head on the cabin ceiling.

"Rise and shine, superkids!" boomed Amanda's cheery voice. She slept in her own room, which adjoined our cabin.

"Ugh." Melanie rubbed her eyes. "What time is it?"

"Five-fifteen," grumbled Casey. *"A.m.!"*

"Yes," said Amanda. "Since it's the first full day, I let you guys sleep in. Tomorrow I'll come in at five sharp."

"Why?" asked Megan—quite reasonably, I thought. "The brochure says breakfast isn't till eight."

"Right," said Amanda, "and while your opponents are still snoozing, we'll be out training for the cup contest. So move it, ladies!" She poked Melanie, who'd pulled the covers over her head and was trying to go back to sleep. "We've got to be down at the dock in ten minutes to meet the boys."

"Boys?" Suddenly, Melanie wasn't under the blankets anymore. "Quick," she cried, jumping out of bed, "somebody get me a hairbrush!"

The sun was rising over the lake when we reached the dock. I was yawning, Megan's eyes were half closed, and Casey was muttering about what she would do for a nice steamy mug of hot cocoa.

Melanie, on the other hand, was as chipper as could be, her pale, powerful blue eyes sparkling like the sun on the water.

"There they are!" she said, pointing to where a group of boys, led by Simon, was coming out of the woods.

"The boys of Bravery cabin," Amanda announced. "Your teammates."

The boys joined us on the dock, looking just as groggy and sleepy as we did. Simon made the introductions.

He pointed to the stocky boy with red hair and freckles. "This is Sam," he said. "Super name: Slam. He's a powerful one, Sam is. He's got superstrength to spare!"

Sam smiled shyly. "Hey."

31

"This is Alexander," Simon continued, nodding toward the boy I thought looked like a football star. "He's the speedster in the group. Clocked him last night going . . . well, actually I *couldn't* clock him because he was moving too fast!"

Alexander waved and smiled at each of us. Then a weird thing happened: when his eyes met mine, I felt a strange little jolt. Not the heart-fluttery kind like when I looked at Josh Devlin, the cutest boy in my school; this jolt made me feel like I had just made a very important connection. I figured it probably had to do with our having the same power.

"This chap is Dave," Simon went on, indicating the third Bravery member, the tall, lanky boy who'd offered to bring Howie some s'mores the night before. "Dave's power is the ability to stretch himself to great lengths."

To demonstrate, Dave spit on his index finger, then reached his arm around Simon, beyond Sam, and past Alexander, all the way to where Howie was hovering alone at the edge of the dock. I noticed that Melanie couldn't seem to take her eyes off the stretchy kid. He noticed her, too, and winked; then, with a mischievous grin, he stuck his finger into Howie's ear and gave him a wet willie. It was

harmless, of course, the kind of silly, gross things boys do to their buddies all the time. But Howie was so startled he toppled over the edge of the dock and landed with a splash in the lake.

Dave simply stretched his arm even farther, reached into the water, and fished Howie out, depositing him safely on the dock.

"This," said Simon, sighing, "is Howie."

"Sorry, pal," said Dave, pulling his

arm back to its natural length. "Didn't mean to scare ya. Just goofin' around."

"What's your power, Howie?" Amanda asked.

I heard Simon mutter "Good question" under his breath. My cabinmates, who already knew the situation from listening to Mr. Hunt's conversation with Simon, looked from me to Howie, then back at me. Howie wiggled his eyebrows at me, clearly remembering that I'd told him not to let on about not having superpowers. He'd obviously kept quiet overnight, but I couldn't see any way of bluffing his way out now, not in front of Amanda and Simon. So I shrugged and gave him a supersympathetic look, hoping he'd understand that it meant "You'll have to tell the truth, bud."

"The truth," Howie said, "is that I don't have one. Yet."

"But his grandpa is super," I put in quickly. "And chances are Howie will be getting his powers any day."

I held my breath, hoping the boys wouldn't pitch a fit about bunking with a non-Super. I was relieved when Alexander just shrugged.

"No biggie," he said.

"Yeah," said Dave. "I'm kind of a power newbie myself, since I just got mine a couple of weeks ago."

Sam gave Howie a high five. "It's cool by me, dude. Let me know if I can lift anything for ya."

I could have hugged each one of them!

"Let's choose our team captains, shall we?" said Simon. "We'll put it to a vote."

I was flattered when my cabinmates unanimously chose me. The boys picked Alexander.

Simon came over to me and patted my back. "Congratulations," he said, then lowered his voice so only I could hear. "I hope you don't let the fact that Alexander is faster than you are get you down."

"How do you know he's faster than I am?" I asked, feeling stung.

"Well, he's a *boy*. . . ."

I raised my eyebrows. "What does that have to do with anything?"

"Sorry," said Simon. "Guess I hit a nerve. We'll just have to see who's faster, won't we?"

Anger prickled inside me. "Yes, we will."

"Let's get started," Amanda was saying. "Breakfast is at eight, so we've only got two and a half hours."

It was the longest two and a half hours of my life!

CHAPTER 5

THE Intrepids and the Bravery boys trudged into the mess hall at 8:01 and slumped onto the narrow benches on either side of one long wooden table.

"That was worse than gym class," Megan observed, dropping her head onto the table.

We'd trained for every second of those two and a half hours, and, super or not, we were exhausted. We'd done sit-ups, push-ups, chin-ups, we stretched (Dave liked that part) and ran, and then we stretched and ran some more.

"That was like gym class times one *billion*," Casey clarified. "Like advanced-placement gym class. No . . . it was like turbo gym class. That was like *atomic* gym."

"Hey, I *know* a kid called Atomic Jim," said Sam. "He's in the Valiant cabin. He glows in the dark, and none of his bunkmates can get any sleep."

"Those push-ups!" Alexander let out a groan. "My biceps are on fire!"

"Melanie," I said calmly, "quit looking at Alexander's arms. You're burning a hole in the sleeve of his polo."

"Sorry," said Melanie, turning her eyes away. "I didn't even realize what I was doing, I'm in so much pain—I've got, like, a zillion blisters from all that running, and I think I'm getting shin splints."

"That's what I like about flying," said Megan. "It's low impact. No impact, actually."

I glanced down to the far end of the table, where Howie was seated. His cheeks were a little pink, and the hair around his face was damp with sweat. But other than that, he looked perfectly fine.

"Howie, how come you aren't as worn out as we are?" I asked.

"Because," said Howie, "you guys went all out right from the get-go. I, on the other hand, paced myself."

My cabinmates and I exchanged glances; so did the Bravery boys. We had attacked all of Amanda and Simon's tasks at full force. I suppose we thought we'd look less than super if we didn't. We'd actually outsupered ourselves in our efforts to impress both the counselors and each other.

"Slow and steady, that's how I did it," said Howie. "After all, exercise is only beneficial if you obey your limits."

"You know something?" said Alexander, flashing a crooked grin around the group. "He's right."

The others agreed; Mega-Megan nodded and Casey gave Howie a thumbs-up.

"Listen, team," Alexander said in a take-charge voice. "I know this morning was tough and we're all feeling beat. But it's only gonna get tougher." He thumped his fist on the table, and his eyes turned serious. "I don't know about you guys, but I really want to win this Courageous Cup. I say we all work as hard as we can to make that happen. We'll pace ourselves, like Howie said, but we won't back down from anything! We'll give it our all. We'll do anything we have to do to be the best. And I mean all of us."

"Jeesh," whispered Megan. "He may be cute, but he's awfully bossy."

"Alexander," said Sam. "We get it. We all want to win."

Alexander suddenly looked embarrassed. He cleared his throat, recovering his cool. "Right. Of course. We all want to win."

A moment of awkward silence passed. My stomach growled, reminding me how hungry I was. I saw Simon on the far side of the mess hall, where the kitchen staff had set up a hearty breakfast buffet. He seemed to be eyeing each selection with great interest—the scrambled eggs, the sausage patties, the pancakes and maple syrup.

Probably calculating the nutritional value of everything, I told myself. *Making a list of what he wants us to eat.*

"Those pancakes smell great," Melanie observed, gazing longingly in the direction of the buffet. "I'd love some, but I think my legs are too tired to walk that far."

"No problem," said Dave, stretching his arm the fifty or so feet across the dining hall. He guided his hand between two campers who were standing in line. "'Scuse me," he called, picking up a serving of pancakes.

"Hey, does that count as cutting in line?" I joked.

"Nope," said Dave. "Cutting is rude. I'd never do that." He turned to Melanie. "Maple syrup?"

Melanie beamed. "Yes, please."

Dave stretched out his other arm, picked up the near-empty syrup pitcher, and poured the last of the sticky stuff over the stack of pancakes.

"You could have left some for the rest of us," huffed the next camper in line, who was holding a plate of waffles.

"Sorry," called Dave, placing the plate on the table in front of Melanie.

"Thanks," breathed Melanie. "That was awesome."

Megan, Casey, and I giggled.

"I guess the rest of us are going to have to walk," teased Sam.

We all stood up gingerly on our sore legs and headed for the buffet. On the way, Alexander pulled me aside.

"About Howie not having his powers . . . ," he began in a low voice. "I think it might be a problem."

"Wait a minute," I said, frowning. "Just because Howie isn't the super-est superkid at this camp doesn't mean he's a problem." I remembered Simon's comment about Alexander's being faster than me and I became even more defensive. "I mean, we all know how much you want to win, thanks to your little speech back there, but if you think you're going to kick my friend Howie off our team—"

"Hold on . . . easy there." Alexander held up his hands to stop me; his grin returned. "Who said anything about kicking him off the team? Not me."

It was true. He hadn't said that. I felt myself flush with embarrassment. "I thought that's what you were getting at."

Alexander shook his head. "What I was going to say was that I'm afraid that if things get too rough during the contest, Howie might get scared, or worse—hurt. And I don't want to see that happen. *That's* what I was getting at."

"Oh." I looked down at my sneakers, feeling like a complete jerk. "That's really nice of you."

"I was thinking, since you and I are cocaptains, we should make it a point to look out for him."

"Yeah. I think that's a good idea, Alexander."

"Thanks," he said. "Oh, and one more thing. Call me Zander."

ZANDER?

Zander, who has superspeed. Like me.

Zander. With a *Z*.

Like Zelda . . . Zip . . . and Zoe.

I gasped, throwing my hand up to cover my mouth.

"Whoa," he said, obviously confused by my reaction. "It's really not that big a deal. If the nickname bothers you that much, you can keep calling me Alexander. Honest, I don't mind!"

His misunderstanding made me laugh. "No," I said. "It's not that. It's not that at all."

He was looking at me with a puzzled expression. I took a deep breath.

"Uh, Zander . . . exactly how much do you know about your family history?"

Before he could answer, four girls came hurrying over. I recognized them as the campers from the Fearless cabin.

"Hi," said the red-haired one.

I'd met her the night before at the campfire. Her name was Sunny; her superpower was the ability to control the weather. For some reason, she was holding a brand-new bottle of ketchup, and she was smiling like crazy at Zander.

"Hi," said Zander.

"We were wondering if you could help us out," she said, a giggle in her voice. "Could you open this ketchup for us? The cap is really, really tight."

"Sure," said Zander. He took the bottle and twisted the cap effortlessly. It opened with a little pop.

"Oh, *thank* you," crooned one of the other Fearless campers.

"We're so grateful," said another.

I rolled my eyes. They were making it sound as if the future of the universe depended on getting that bottle of ketchup opened.

"No problem," said Zander, with that crooked grin of his.

Sunny giggled. "Well, I'll see you around camp," she said, batting her eyelashes a few times.

Under ordinary circumstances, a girl's batting her eyelashes at a boy would be considered standard flirting behavior, but this flirty girl had the power to control the weather. The motion of her eyelashes sent a near-hurricane-force wind blowing through the mess hall, sending tablecloths and paper napkins flying around the room.

Sunny giggled again. "Ooops. My bad." She walked off, whispering with her cabinmates.

I looked at Zander, trying not to crack up.

"What? I was just being nice to some fellow campers."

"You opened a bottle of ketchup for her."

"So?"

I rolled my eyes. "Zander . . . they're superheroes. They have superstrength. I think they were more than capable of opening a puny little bottle of ketchup."

"Oh." He was looking puzzled again. "So why do you think Sunny asked me to do it?"

This time, I did crack up. "Never mind. Let's just go get breakfast."

Zander followed me to the breakfast buffet, still looking confused. I couldn't wait to tell Megan and Casey what I'd just discovered: All boys are completely oblivious. Even the super ones.

CHAPTER

7

SUNDAY, Day 2
8:00 a.m. Breakfast

9:00 a.m. MORNING ACTIVITIES (Elective)

Aquatic Rescue Technique
Lessons include swimming in tsunamis and extended breath holding during underwater disasters.
Location: Lake

Soaring Seminar: Intro to Flying
For those who can already soar and those who hope to develop this power in the future. Followed by a general discussion of international airspace regulations and tips for avoiding airsickness.
Location: Field House rooftop

Proper Table Manners for Heroes
Learn how to dine in polite circles without bending, melting, or otherwise destroying the silverware.
Location: Dining Hall

Fire-Breathing Workshop
Superpower or parlor trick? You be the judge. Come learn how to spit flames, a skill that comes in handy not only during heroic missions but at weenie roasts as well. Please bring your own hot dogs.
Location: As far away from the trees as possible

Basic Navigational Skills
Tried-and-true "trailblazing" methods to help heroes get where they're going without the use of state-of-the-art Federation technology.
Location: Entrance to Main Lodge, where maps will be distributed prior to wilderness excursion

Arts and Crafts (Self-explanatory)
Location: Main Lodge, Rec Room

1:00 p.m. Lunch (for those who did not take part in the fire-breathing weenie roast)
Location: Mess Hall

2:00 p.m. Free Time

2:30 p.m. AFTERNOON ACTIVITIES (Required)
The afternoon is reserved for intensive team training.
Location: TBD at your counselors' discretion

6:00 p.m. Dinner

After breakfast, we decided which workshops to do.

"Who wants to check out the aquatic rescue seminar?" I asked.

"I do!" cried Casey. "I love swimming. I can hear the fish! You might think they don't say much, but whoa, buddy, some of those trout never shut up."

Dave said he'd come along with Casey and me, although he didn't really need to improve his swimming, since there wasn't a body of water on this or any other planet that was too deep for him; he simply had to stretch his legs to touch the bottom and stretch his neck to keep his head above water.

"The real reason I want to hang out at the lake," he confided, "is so I can work on my tan."

Megan was going to attend the soaring seminar. The counselor teaching the class, Skylar, had invited her to demonstrate her power for the future flyers and to get some one-on-one coaching. Zander was going to check out the fire-breathing class, and Sam couldn't wait to get to arts and crafts.

"I promised my little sister I'd make her a change purse," he told us.

"I'll go to arts and crafts, too," said Melanie. "Maybe I can give a little woodburning demonstration. Like I can burn people's names into Popsicle sticks or something."

46

Simon, who was just coming out of the dining hall, stopped and smiled. "Burning Popsicle sticks. That's a great idea, Mel. Let everyone know what a fiery talent you've got there."

Melanie blushed at Simon's compliment. "Thanks."

"What about you, Howie?" I asked, hoping he wouldn't say he was going to try flying.

"Navigational skills," he said.

I relaxed, because that one did sound like the safest choice for a non-Super.

We wished each other luck and went off to our separate activities.

After the seminar, I had lunch with Casey and Megan and Melanie (grilled cheese sandwiches and tomato soup—yum!), then went to meet Howie at the dock. He looked relaxed and happy, so I figured he'd had a good morning.

"How was your navigation class?" I asked.

"Amazing!" His eyes were wide, and he couldn't seem to stop smiling. "We learned how to plot longitude and latitude. We went over old-fashioned map-reading skills, because it's always good to be familiar with the basics. We even learned to use the stars as a guide."

"Stars?" I looked up into the bright blue sun-drenched sky. "There aren't any stars out now."

"They're out in Japan," he said.

I gulped. "You went to *Japan*?"

Howie nodded. "One of the counselors—his name is Launch—has this incredible rocket-type thingy. It's kind of like the space shuttle, only way more high-tech and lots faster. We flew to Japan in thirteen minutes flat. That's where we learned about navigating by following the stars."

"Cool."

"I can't believe my grandpa has been doing this sort of thing his whole life! I can't wait to get home and ask him about it! So, how was your workshop?"

"Excellent," I said. "The instructor, Puff, has superpowered lungs. She was able to create giant waves in the lake just by swimming out to the middle and blowing on the surface."

"Neat."

"Now, how about that canoe ride?"

We put on our life jackets (rules are rules, even at supercamp) and stepped into a canoe. Howie handed me a paddle and we were off. The lake was a little choppy—a residual effect of the waves Puff had created—so we didn't have to paddle too hard. As we let the long, narrow boat rock gently across the water, I told Howie everything. About my twelfth birthday and how I couldn't get my ears pierced. About Grandpa Zack showing me his scrapbooks in the garage and telling me that I had Super genes, even though my parents were Ordinaries. I told him about the Superhero Federation handbook and the exam, and how important it is to keep everything a secret from non-Supers.

"That's the crazy thing," I said. "All this time I've been struggling to keep my secret about being superpowered. Now we're trying to keep it on the down-low that you're *not* superpowered. I know your cabinmates were cool and everything, but I'm not sure how everyone else would react to having a non-super staying here. And once camp is over, it'll be such a relief to have a superbuddy right next door. You and I can talk about this stuff anytime we want, as long as we're careful. Maybe once your powers kick in, we can go on missions together."

Howie grinned. "Yeah!"

"You'll get a supersuit," I told him. "That part's really cool. Mine's pink and green, and I've got boots and a mask, too."

"I bet it's really aerodynamic. And the fabric must be some specially formulated synthetic. Are the boots hydraulic?" Howie was *so* into technical stuff, I sometimes wondered how he managed to store all of it in his brain. I mean, his head was the same size as mine, so what did he do, use his arms and legs for memory storage?

"I have no idea, but I've got this really incredible communication device. You'll get one, too, eventually, so you can touch base with the Federation whenever you need to. There's this really cool dispatcher guy who helped me out on my last mission. His name is Thatcher."

"Thatcher the Dispatcher?" said Howie.

I giggled. "Yeah. Pretty funny, huh?"

"I wonder what my power will be."

"Could be anything," I said. "You'll probably develop some degree of superstrength, since everybody seems to. But beyond that . . . who knows?"

"I'd like to be able to disappear," he said. "Or read people's minds."

We sat quietly for a few minutes, just enjoying the calming motion of the canoe, the sun on our faces, the light breeze.

Until we heard the whistle.

I shaded my eyes and looked back toward the beach. Amanda was standing on the sand, hands on hips, blasting impatiently on her whistle.

"Training time," I said.

Howie and I dipped our paddles into the water and headed back to shore.

"Thanks for telling me all this, Zoe," said Howie.

I noticed that there was a shine in his eyes and I could tell that he just couldn't wait to get his powers.

I smiled. Who could blame him?

CHAPTER

8

FOR afternoon training, Simon and Amanda worked us even harder than they had that morning. We started out with basic stretching to warm up, then moved into an aerobic workout. The boys got a little silly and started doing the can-can, which made everyone laugh. Then we got down to business with weight training. Of course, we didn't use actual weights, we used camp stuff—kayaks, picnic tables. Howie was the official cheerleader and did a great job cheering us on. Then the counselors led us a mile or so through the woods to a clearing.

"You've exercised your muscles," said Simon in his crisp English accent. "Now it's time to calm your minds. We're going to take this time to sit quietly and meditate on the journey to victory, the personal satisfaction of performing to your utmost and surpassing all others."

I had no idea what he meant, but after the workout, the idea of sitting around with my eyes closed and breathing deeply sure sounded good to me.

Simon showed us how to sit in the lotus position and told us that chanting would help us connect with our inner superhero.

For a while, we just sat there humming and enjoying the warmth of the day.

"Oops," said Megan.

I opened one eye and saw that she was still in lotus position, but she was hovering ten feet in the air. Sam opened his eyes and started cracking up.

Megan lowered herself back to the grass, drifting downward as gently as a snowflake. "I like meditating," she said.

"Me too," said Dave. "Being super puts a lot of pressure on a kid. It's nice to just sit and zone out."

Casey frowned. "I'd like it a whole lot better if I didn't keep picking up conversations taking place back at camp. I keep tuning in to the Fearless cabin."

"I'm not surprised," said Melanie. "Those girls are always yakking about something."

"What are they saying?" I asked. Remembering that Casey had said she only used her powers in times of dire need, I added, "It could be about the competition!"

Casey pushed her hair behind her ear and got a look of concentration on her face. We waited.

"They're talking about . . . about . . ." She shot a glance at Zander. "About you!"

Zander looked surprised and embarrassed. "Me?"

Casey nodded and kept listening. After a while, she rolled her eyes. "Oh, brother."

"What are they saying?" asked Dave.

"They're saying," Casey reported, "that Zander is the coolest boy at Camp Courageous and that he's majorly hunk-a-licious, and they're daring each other to ask him for his communication-device call digits."

"You're supposed to be meditating," Simon reminded us from the other side of the circle. "Reflecting on your goals, celebrating your own powerfulness, recalling the joy of individual greatness . . ."

"Actually," said Amanda, "this is better. They're learning about each other instead, which is very bonding. It's a great team-building exercise." She turned to Sam. "Tell us a little more about your power."

"It's superstrength, but off the charts, basically. I've been tested by the Superhero Federation and found to possess ten times the strength of any adult hero on record. I'd demonstrate for you," he said apologetically, "but I'm on restricted usage. I can only use my power to its full extent in an emergency."

"So how strong are you?" Dave asked.

"Let's put it this way," said Sam. "If the Leaning Tower of Pisa ever does topple over, I'll be the one holding it up until they can secure it again."

"Wow," said Dave. "That's strong." He turned to Melanie and gave her a flirty look. "It must be cool being able to light fires with your eyes."

"She sure lit his fire," Zander whispered to me. I giggled.

"It is," said Mel. "In fact, you know the torch they use to kick off the Courageous Cup contest?" She smiled broadly. "Battlin' Bertram has asked me to light it!"

"Mel, that rocks!" cried Casey.

"You go, girl," said Sam, clapping.

We all congratulated her on the honor of being chosen to light the Courageous Cup flame, and I could tell Amanda was pleased with our show of support. The way she was watching us hang out was a little unnerving, but if getting to know my new friends went under the heading "team building" as far as Amanda was concerned, that was okay with me.

"I have an idea," said Simon. He seemed a little testy, as if he was insulted that we'd blown off his meditation idea. "Let's put our two speedsters to a real test." He stood up and motioned for Zander and me to join him at the edge of the clearing. "How about a race?"

Sam began punching a fist in the air, chanting, "Race, race, race . . ."

Zander was up on his feet in a flash.

"I don't know about this," said Amanda.

Neither did I. I'd never raced anyone since I'd become super, and I wasn't exactly thrilled about going up against the *other* fastest kid on the planet. Not that I'd ever been a sore loser, but I didn't want to make myself look bad.

Simon raised his eyebrows at Amanda. "I thought you were the competitive sort."

"I am," said Amanda. "When it comes to beating the other teams. But Zander and Zoe are teammates, not opponents."

Simon waved off her concern. "You'll run to camp," he suggested, pointing into the dense trees and scraggly underbrush surrounding our grassy clearing. "Straight there and back—two miles, give or take."

"I can do that in ten seconds," Zander boasted.

I gave him a challenging smile. "Then I guess I'll just have to do it in nine."

"Okay, speedsters," said Simon. "You'll find Bertram's car in the parking lot, a red luxury sedan. That can be your landmark, so you know you've gone the same distance. Run through the woods and down the main path of camp to the parking lot, and touch the car. Then turn around and run back the same way. Ready? On your mark, get set . . ."

His whistle blared and we were off, moving almost as quickly as light.

It was a thrilling feeling, running at my full, amazing speed with Zander right there, pumping along beside me. In the shadows of the woods, we hopped over fallen trees and ducked low branches, all without missing a step. I couldn't see Zander—he was a shimmer of motion—but I could feel him there. When camp was in sight, we headed for the winding dirt footpath and zoomed toward our destination. The shapes of cabins and the colors of the campground whizzed past in a woodsy blur.

The parking lot was in my sight in no time; Bertram's red car shone in the sun. Zander and I were heading for it shoulder to shoulder. I was having so much fun sharing this super experience with Zander, but there was no doubt about it—I wanted to win!

"No way are you going to beat me," Zander cried, turning on more power as we closed in on the car.

The swell of energy that exploded from his body when he surged ahead of me was so strong that it actually knocked me over. I was pushed sideways by the invisible force, and I lost my footing and hit the ground. I was still moving at supervelocity, and the momentum of my own speed sent me rolling across the gravel lot, bumping my head, twisting my ankle, and scraping my bare knees before I skidded to a stop.

Zander was still running. For a moment, I didn't think he

knew I'd fallen, but when he reached the bumper of Bertram's car, he paused and looked at me sprawled on the ground. Our eyes met and again I felt that jolt, that spark that said we were somehow connected.

I was sure he would come over and make sure I was okay.

But he turned away from the car and kept running.

I caught up to him halfway through the woods. My knees could have used some Band-Aids, but my ankle was okay, though it had hurt for the first few strides. Still, I was so angry with Zander for leaving me behind that breaking both legs wouldn't have stopped me from chasing him at top superspeed.

"Hey!" I shouted through the windy rush of our combined speed.

I brought my hand down on his shoulder and yanked hard until we came to a stop, our heels digging deep ruts in the ground.

"What's wrong with you?" I demanded. "You knock me over and then just leave me there? You don't even stop to ask if I'm okay? What do you call that?"

"I call it a race," he snapped.

I glared at him. "A *friendly* race."

"No such thing."

My mouth dropped open. "Zander!"

Suddenly, the bluster went out of him. "I'm sorry," he said, and I could tell he meant it. "You're right. I should have stopped to help you. But all I could think about was winning."

"It's okay," I said. "I guess in all the excitement you kind of lost your head. I just don't see why it would be so important to you to win some silly little race—I mean, this isn't the cup contest."

"I know. But in my family, winning is *everything*. Even if it is just a silly little race, I have to win."

"Says who?"

"Says . . ." He looked away. "My grandfather."

That's when I remembered what I'd been thinking that morning. "Zander, tell me about your family. The Super side, that is."

He thought for a moment. "Well, I don't know much about any of my other Super relatives except that my mom and her father, my grandpa Zeb, are both Supers."

I tried to remember the family tree I'd seen in my grandpa Zack's scrapbook. My great-grandmother Zelda had had an uncle, Zeke, who was an Ordinary. But Zeke's grandson was super . . . and his name was Zeb.

Zack and Zeb were first cousins.

Which meant that Zack's granddaughter and Zeb's grandson were cousins, too.

I smiled at Zander.

He cocked an eyebrow at me. "What?"

"I think we should *walk* back to the clearing, Zander. There's something I have to tell you."

CHAPTER

9

"**SO** we're cousins?" said Zander.

"Yup. Distant cousins, but still cousins."

We were walking slowly back to the clearing through the woods; I'd told him everything I learned from the family tree in Grandpa's album.

"I wonder why no one ever told me about you," he said, pushing aside a branch for me, then ducking under it himself. "Or your grandpa."

"I do, too," I said. "When I found out about you, I was pretty psyched. I meant to ask my grandpa, but then there was this whole big mess with Electra Allbright and I guess I forgot."

"Electra Allbright?" said Zander. "The comic-book author?"

"Yeah," I said. "But that's a whole other story! I'll check with my grandpa tonight and see if I can find out why you and I have never met."

When we returned to the clearing, everyone seemed confused.

"For two kids with superspeed, you sure are a couple of slow-pokes," joked Sam. "What happened to being back in ten seconds?"

"Yeah," said Dave. "It took you ten *minutes.*"

"So nobody won?" asked Megan.

I laughed. "I guess you can say we tied."

"Yeah," said Dave. "For last place."

"We should be heading back to camp," said Simon. His lips were pursed like he'd been sucking a lemon; he was obviously disappointed we hadn't taken the race more seriously. I was beginning to wonder if we'd ended up with the two most competitive counselors on the planet—and what they might do to us if we didn't win the Courageous Cup.

"Too bad Howie doesn't have a power yet," said Casey. I noticed she was staring at him with a dreamy look in her eyes. "I bet when he gets one, it'll be the coolest."

"I don't mind, really," said Howie. "It'll happen when it happens. For now, I'm just glad to have such terrific teammates."

"That's the spirit, Howie," said Amanda. "It's what the Courageous Cup is all about. Something all heroes need to remember. Ego can be a real problem for a superhero. Have you guys ever heard the story of the Sweep?"

Simon stepped forward, cutting her off. "I don't think we have time for a story, Amanda," he said. "We've got to get moving. More work to do back at camp, strategies to plan, you know."

"Amanda can tell us the story on the hike back," Dave suggested. "This sounds interesting."

"Good idea," said Amanda.

As the team fell in line to make our way back to camp, she began. "Not long ago, the Sweep was one of the most celebrated young heroes of his generation. He didn't develop his powers until late—around his fourteenth birthday—but when they showed themselves, no one could believe it. Sweep was one of those rare heroes who only come along once in an eon. . . . He possessed every single power there was. Made a clean sweep, if you will. That was how he got his name."

"*Every* power?" I echoed, amazed.

"Well, almost every power. He could freeze things with his breath and shrink things by shooting beams from his eyes, and he could hold his breath for hours at a time. He was a flyer, like Megan, and he had superstrength in the extreme, just like Sam. He could melt things like Mel, he had superhearing like Casey, and he could stretch like Dave. The only power he didn't have was superspeed. And boy, did that make him mad."

"So?" said Howie. "I mean, no offense to Zoe and Zander, superspeed is certainly impressive, not to mention useful. But he had so many other things going for him, he should have been happy with those."

"I agree," said Amanda. "But Sweep was an egomaniac, and he didn't like to share the glory. Whenever there was a mission that called for superspeed, he had to be partnered up, and that made him crazy. Well, at that time, there was a super-villain called the Haste Maker. He had built a machine that would significantly speed up the rate at which the Earth was spinning on its axis."

"Which would have put an end to life as we know it," said Howie. I caught his eye just in time, guessing he was about to launch into a lecture on gravitational force, and gave my head the tiniest shake. He shut his mouth.

"That was his plan," said Amanda. "Well, the Federation knew young Sweep was the best hero for the job, so they sent him after the Haste Maker. He was able to overpower the villain . . ."

"No doubt it required an act of unparalleled might on the part of the Sweep," Simon put in.

". . . but a terrible thing happened. The Haste Maker managed to start up his machine the moment before the Sweep captured him, and once the contraption was on, there was no way to turn it off."

"What did Sweep do?"

"He called in to the Federation to tell them the Haste Maker had been apprehended, but he didn't alert them to the fact that the machine was already working. He knew that all he had to do was tell the Feds to send a hero with superspeed to run around the equator in the opposite direction of the Earth's rotation—that would have thwarted the action of the machine, keeping the spin speed stabilized until the Federation techies could arrive and disengage the Haste Maker's machine. But the Sweep wanted to solve this problem alone, without the help of any other Super. He wanted all the glory for himself. So he flew to the equator and began to run . . ."

"But he couldn't run fast enough," I said.

"Right," said Amanda.

"Is anyone interested in heading over to the canteen for an ice cream sandwich?" asked Simon.

"What happened next?" asked Zander.

"Well," said Amanda, "eventually, the Federation figured out what was going wrong, and they sent a hero with superspeed to do the running. The Sweep was tried by a jury of Super peers and forever banned from the Superhero Federation." She shook her head. "It was a shame. He had so much to give, and because of his ego, he threw it all away."

"I'm glad we don't have anybody like the Sweep on our team," said Casey.

"Yeah," said Sam. "What a loser." He made an L with his thumb and forefinger and held it to his forehead. "Looooo-ser!"

"Enough about the Sweep," Simon said briskly. "I mean, let's not dwell on something so negative."

"Simon's right," said Amanda. "It's a pretty sad story."

"Hey, I don't have superspeed, either, but I'll bet I can beat you guys to an ice cream sandwich," said Howie, tugging his backpack higher on his shoulder and breaking into a run. Everyone laughed and gave chase—though I noticed Zander didn't break into superspeed, and neither did I.

As I brought up the rear, glad to give my scorching sneakers a rest from running at full speed, I thought about Howie. Mr. Hunt had hoped being at camp would jump-start his grandson's powers, but so far, there was no sign of them. Howie seemed okay with that, but I wondered if deep down he felt left out. I knew that if I were in his position, I would want to be doing all the super things the rest of us were getting to try. On the other hand, I was just glad that we were all getting along so well, becoming not only teammates but also friends. No one seemed to mind that Howie wasn't a proper Super yet—Casey seemed to mind least of all, though I wasn't sure Howie had noticed. All in all, I couldn't have wished to be on a better team.

All of a sudden, I had a really good feeling about the Courageous Cup.

After dinner we hung around in the rec room. Casey and I played Ping-Pong against Zander and Dave, but Dave kept using his stretching power and never missed a single point. Melanie kept score and giggled like crazy every time Dave did something stretchy. Girls from the other cabins kept trying to get Zander's attention, which made Megan and me crack up. Howie and Casey played Crazy Eights, while Sam put the finishing touches on the knitted wallet he'd started for his sister in arts and crafts.

Then some of the kids from the Justice cabin suggested a game of flashlight tag, and the next thing we knew, we were all outside running around, dodging flashlight beams and having a blast. It was especially cool that some of the campers didn't even need flashlights because they could shine light rays from their fingertips or eyes. In the end, a girl named Shannon (Super name: Shadow) won the game because she had night vision, the power to see in the dark.

Howie and I met up under a tall pine tree.

"That was fun!" I said.

"Yeah," said Howie. "The kids at this camp are great."

"They think you're great, too," I told him. "That one kid was really grateful to you for fixing his flashlight when it went out."

"It wasn't a big deal," said Howie modestly. "When he told me he had the power to absorb people's energy, I figured out that he was probably absorbing the power of the flashlight batteries. All he had to do was shift out of his Super mode and the flashlight worked fine." He looked up into the evening sky, where dark clouds were drifting in to cover the early stars. "I'm just glad we got the game in before the rain begins," he said.

Casey, Sam, Megan, and Zander joined us under the tree.

"Has anyone seen Mel?" Megan asked.

I looked around and noticed she was missing.

"And where's Dave?" Sam wondered.

Suddenly, Casey began to giggle. When I realized what she was thinking, I started laughing, too.

"I bet they're off holding hands somewhere," said Zander, rolling his eyes.

Sam made a pretend gagging sound. "Gross."

"I think it's kinda cute," I said. "They like each other, and—"

Suddenly, Howie held up his hand. "Shhh." He looked concerned.

"What is it?" asked Casey.

"Does anyone else smell smoke?" Howie said.

We all sniffed. I felt a stab of panic.

"I do," I said.

"It's coming from that direction," said Sam, pointing. "C'mon!"

We all took off; Zander and I automatically went into Super mode and bolted ahead. Once we crossed out of the main section of camp, we could see the flames, bright orange against the inky black trees.

Bravery cabin was on fire!

I'd never been so scared in my life. All I could think was that there might be someone inside the cabin. We hadn't seen Dave since supper. The fire seemed to have just started; so far, only the front-porch timbers had caught. Thick smoke twisted up into the sky.

"What do we do?" I cried. "Zander, are you fireproof?"

"Not that I know of," he shouted.

The others caught up to us.

"Hold still, everybody!" said Casey. She pushed her hair behind her ear and tilted her head toward the cabin. "I don't hear anyone inside," she reported. "The cabin is empty, thank goodness."

"We need water!" hollered Sam.

"Has anyone seen Puff? She could suck up a bunch of lake water and spray it!" I suggested.

"What about Sunny?" said Melanie. "She could make it rain!"

"She went with Puff and Amanda," said Casey. "She's on extra chores after the Mess Hall fog incident."

"I heard her telling Simon that she and Amanda were going into town for supplies," said Casey.

Suddenly, I remembered the clouds Howie had pointed out. It wasn't raining yet, but maybe with some superhelp . . .

"Howie," I said, my voice anxious, "do you think there's any way we could get those clouds to rain right now? Maybe if Megan were to fly up into the clouds—could she do something to make it start?"

"Yes!" said Howie. "If she flies straight into that big cloud and starts moving the moisture inside it around, she can make it rain. Basically, the cloud drops need to bump into each other in order to grow big enough to fall as raindrops. So she'll have to move fast once she's inside."

Megan looked serious. "I can try," she said.

"Take me with you," said Zander. "You get us up there and I can help you mix up the moisture at superspeed."

Megan grabbed Zander's hand and together they shot up toward the low-hanging cloud.

I crossed my fingers. The flames were growing bigger, and the smell of the burning cabin was tickling the inside of my nose. By now, other campers and counselors had noticed the smoke and had come running. Simon pushed his way to the front of the crowd.

Seconds later, the rain began.

"They did it!" said Sam.

The rain fell in fast, heavy drops that instantly became a deluge, dousing the fire. The flames sputtered and sizzled, then died, leaving the charred porch railings black and smoldering.

Megan and Zander landed moments later; they were both still damp.

I ran over to them. "That was awesome, you guys."

"You were the one who thought of the clouds, Zoe," said Megan, pushing her wet hair out of her eyes.

"And Howie was the one who knew what to do to make it rain," said Casey.

Zander walked over to Howie and shook his hand. "Nice going, pal."

Howie grinned.

"All right, campers," said Simon, waving the onlookers away. "Nothing to see here. Everything turned out fine."

I was about to walk away, but Simon put a firm hand on my shoulder. "Not you guys," he said, looking around at our group. "You stay."

While we waited for the others to leave, Howie took off his jacket and offered it to Megan, who was shivering in her wet sweatshirt. When everyone was gone, Simon said in a low, somber voice, "Where's Melanie?"

I shot a glance at Casey—neither of us was giggling now. Melanie would be mortified if we told Simon that she and Dave were off enjoying a moonlight walk together.

"Campers . . . this is important. We have to account for everyone. I need to know where Melanie is."

"I'm right here," came a voice from behind us.

We all whirled around to see Melanie and Dave emerging from the path that led to the lake. They were looking a tiny bit pink-cheeked and were walking at least three feet apart, like they wanted to make it perfectly clear that they *were not holding hands.* But then again, three feet was no distance at all for Dave's superstretchy arms. . . .

"Whoa! What happened?" Dave asked, taking in the smoldering cabin.

Simon lowered his eyes. "Perhaps you can tell us," he said, a note of sadness in his voice. When he looked up again, his gaze was fixed on Melanie. "It looks like someone set the Bravery cabin on fire," he explained.

It took a moment for his accusation to sink in. When it did, Melanie's blue eyes grew round. "Do you think I did this?" she gasped, her voice trembling. "I would never, ever do anything like this, honest!"

"I know you wouldn't," Simon said reassuringly. He stepped toward her and put a hand on her shoulder. "Not on purpose. But, well . . ." He paused. "I know how tricky it can be for beginner Supers to keep their powers in check."

Everyone looked away, and I was sure they were remembering how Mel had accidentally singed Zander's shirtsleeve that morning. Not to mention what she'd done to Amanda's whistle at the first training session.

68

"Especially," Simon went on, "when they've got other things on their minds. Now, I'm not blaming you entirely, Mel." He took a deep breath and let it out slowly. "It's partly my fault, because I saw you two walking by here earlier."

"You did?" said Dave.

Simon gave him a smile. "I should have stopped you, but far be it from me to stand in the way of young love."

Dave and Melanie looked miserable *and* embarrassed.

"Is there any chance," said Simon, his English accent very gentle, "that you accidentally shot a spark out of your eyes when you walked past this cabin?"

I could see Melanie struggling to remember. "I don't know," she admitted. "I guess I can't say for sure whether I did or didn't." She sniffled. "But if I did, I didn't mean to. It's like you said, I wasn't thinking about my power, so maybe it just happened. I could have given the cabin a superstare. I truly don't remember if I did."

"Or if you didn't," Simon added kindly but pointedly. "I guess we'll never know for certain."

Back at the cabin, Melanie went directly to her dresser and began taking clothes out of the drawers.

"What are you doing?" I asked.

"Packing. I'm leaving."

"Why?" asked Megan. "Simon didn't say you had to leave."

"No, he didn't," said Mel. "But I can't trust myself to stay here. The whole place is made of wood . . . the cabins, the picnic tables, the canoes! And let's not forget the millions of trees. I can't risk starting any more fires!"

"But you don't know for sure that you started that one," I reminded her. "An electrical short could have caused it. Or one of the lanterns on the porch could have blown over."

Melanie shook her head. "I just can't take the chance."

Casey looked dismayed. "So you're leaving?"

Melanie nodded. "First thing in the morning. I'll call my folks and tell them I've got really bad poison ivy or malaria or something, and they can come and pick me up."

"We'll miss you," I said.

"I'll miss you, too."

The cabin got very quiet as Melanie continued to pack. I knew that for the moment, at least, there was no danger of my cabinmate's accidentally starting a fire with her eyes . . . because they were filled with glistening tears.

While Megan, Mel, and Casey were getting ready for bed, I dug my communication device out of my backpack and went out onto the porch.

"Central Communications," answered a familiar voice.

"Hey, Thatcher. It's Kid Zoom."

"Zoe! So nice to hear from you. Enjoying camp?"

"Well, we had a pretty scary incident tonight, and now Melanie's leaving."

"Melt is leaving camp?" Thatcher asked, surprised. "That's awful."

"I know. But we can't talk her out of it."

"So what can I do for you, Zoe?"

"Can you patch me through to Grandpa Zack, please?"

"Don't tell me you've run out of underwear already!"

71

"Thatcher!" I laughed. "Boy, you really do know everything, don't you?"

"It's my job."

I waited while the device buzzed and flashed, connecting me to Grandpa's wavelength.

"Zip here."

"Grandpa!"

"Zoe, sweetheart. How are things at Camp Courageous?"

I told him all about the fire, and how I'd thought of the rain clouds and how Howie had taught Megan how to make it rain.

"Howie?" Grandpa interrupted. "Not Howie Hunt?"

"Yep."

"Howie's at Camp Courageous?" Grandpa laughed. "Well, I guess that secret is out. So tell me, when did his powers appear?"

"They didn't, yet. Mr. Hunt forced the counselor to let Howie stay. Don't worry, though, I'm looking out for him."

"Good girl."

"Grandpa, that's not the only secret that's out."

"What do you mean?"

I drew a deep breath. "I met Zander."

There was a long pause.

"Zander," Grandpa said. "Your cousin."

"I saw his name in the family tree and I meant to ask you about him, but I forgot, and then I came to camp and there he was. He didn't know anything about me, or you. I told him the little bit I learned from your scrapbook, but now we're both wondering why we never met, or even heard of each other."

"Zander's grandfather Zeb was my cousin," Grandpa told me. "We grew up together, came into our powers mere weeks

72

apart—we even went to camp together. We were very close. Well, time went on, we grew older, married, and started our families. Gran and I had your dad, and Zeb and his wife, Cheryl, had a daughter, Zia."

"Another *Z*," I said. "Big surprise."

"Zia was a Super."

"Oh. That's nice."

"Well, I thought so. But I never got a chance to tell Zeb that, because as soon as Zia's powers showed themselves, he cut off all ties. I had no idea why. Best I could surmise was that since your dad was not a Super, Zeb didn't feel my family was good enough to associate with his, which had produced two Supers in a row. I never heard from him again. I called him a few times, but the conversations were always very awkward. It was like he had nothing to say to me."

"That's kind of stuck-up," I said.

Grandpa gave a sad chuckle. "I suppose you could call it that. And then Zia got married and she had baby Zander. The only reason I was able to put Zander's name in the family tree was because I read about his birth in the *Superhero News*. And when his powers arrived, around the same time as yours did, there was a whole story about him in the *Superhero News* because he was the third consecutive Super born into that family. That's very unusual. The Federation is making a big fuss over Zander."

"So are the girls in the Fearless cabin," I said.

"Excuse me?"

"Never mind. So Zander and I don't have to keep our family connection on the DL?"

"No, you don't have to keep it on the down-low. I'm glad you found each other. Family is important. Who knows, maybe now

73

Zeb and I will reconnect and I'll finally find out what went wrong between us."

Grandpa and I chatted a few minutes longer about camp stuff: starchy food, creaky bunks, and mosquito bites. He said my mom and dad were missing me like crazy, but he and Gran were keeping them company. When it was time to sign off, he wished me luck in the cup contest.

"See you on visitors' day," I said.

There was a whirring sound, and Thatcher came back on. "All done?" he asked.

"Yep. Thanks, Thatcher."

"No problem, Kid Zoom. Over and out."

I put my communication device in my backpack and headed into the cabin. My cabinmates were already asleep. No wonder—it had been a pretty eventful and exhausting day. I climbed into my bunk and tried to stay awake to enjoy the sounds of the chirping crickets and night breezes, but I was just too tired.

In moments, I was sleeping, too.

CHAPTER 10

WE all got up early to see Melanie off. Casey, Megan, and I walked her to the parking lot, where her grandparents were waiting.

"Write to me," she begged. "Let me know how the contest goes."

After a long group hug, she left.

Sadly we headed back to join Simon and the boys on the sports field for the morning's workout.

"We're going to take a break from the calisthenics," said Amanda. "Today we're going to work on trust-building activities. Zoe, will you and Howie join me over here? Everyone spread out so you can all see."

Howie and I took several steps forward.

"This exercise is called a trust fall," Amanda explained. "Now, Howie, you stand in front of Zoe, with your back to her."

Howie did as he was told, positioning himself about a foot or so in front of me.

"When I count to three, Howie, you just fall backward, and Zoe will catch you."

"What's so hard about that?" asked Sam.

"The fall itself isn't difficult," Amanda said. "It's having complete faith in your partner that takes some doing."

"I trust Zoe," said Howie. "She won't let me fall."

"Then go ahead. Just let yourself drop backward."

Howie didn't even hesitate. He closed his eyes and leaned back. . . . I put my arms out and . . .

The next second, I felt a tickle in my nose and began sneezing wildly.

"Whoa!" said Dave, stretching his arms across the space between us and catching Howie just before he hit the ground.

I gasped. "Oh my gosh, Howie! I'm so sorry."

"No problem," he said. "You would have caught me if you weren't sneezing."

Amanda handed me a tissue, then began pairing up the others. Everyone laughed and joked, but luckily, nobody dropped anyone!

When we were done, we headed back to camp for lunch. I noticed I had some dandelion fluff on my T-shirt.

"A breeze must have blown the fluff at you," said Simon, watching as I brushed the fluff off.

"That must be why I sneezed," I said, shrugging. "I guess even superheroes can have tickly noses. It's a good thing Dave was there to catch Howie."

"It certainly is," Simon agreed.

The boys decided to take a swim before the mess hall opened. As they took off for the lake, I noticed Simon say something to Sam. Sam told the other guys he'd catch up to them and walked away with Simon, deep in conversation.

"Let's go check our mail," Casey suggested, pulling my attention away from Simon and Sam. "My uncle Altitude promised to write me a letter." She giggled. "He's sending it airmail, of course."

"Great," I said. "Let's roll."

"Yeah," said Casey. "Let's go."

"Yeah," said Mega-Megan, hopping up from her bunk. "Let's fly."

It took Casey and me a moment to realize she meant that *literally*.

"Megan, this is awesome!" I cried.

"Glad you're enjoying yourself."

We were arm in arm, a good mile above the camp, soaring against the brilliant blue sky through the occasional cloud, which was nothing more than a cool wisp of misty softness.

We were flying!

Casey had opted to walk, given her last flying experience. I looked down; the cabins were tiny brown dots, and the lake shone like a blue jewel.

It wasn't as though I'd never been airborne before. I'd done plenty of superjumping, blasting off into the atmosphere, coming down several feet away, then springing up again. But jumping was a whole different sensation—fast and athletic.

Flying with Megan gave me a sensation of floating, simply drifting from one place to another. For a supermission, of course, she'd have to turn on some power and really jet, but not today.

We touched down in front of the main lodge, where the mailroom was. I read the stick-on labels that marked the mail slots until I found my name, then pulled out a letter from Emily at soccer camp.

Dear zoe,

Having fun. Miss you Lots.

Soccer camp

Megan was feeling around in her mailbox. "Nothin' for me," she said.

"Me either," said Casey, who'd caught up with us. "So much for airmail."

"Well, I'm happy to share my letter with you guys," I said.

"Great," said Megan. "Read it to us."

As we walked toward the mess hall, I read my note from Emily aloud. We laughed about how she was teaching her cabinmates to choose appropriate fashion accessories that wouldn't interfere with their soccer skills. Then she went on to explain in detail this amazing new game strategy their counselor had taught them, involving some tricky passing moves and even bouncing the ball off their heads.

"I used to love playing soccer," said Casey, "before I got my power. Then I had to quit because I could hear what the other

78

coach was telling his team, and it made me feel like I was cheating. It was kind of sad. I had some nice friends on my soccer team."

"Yeah, I know what you mean. I really have to watch my speed when I'm doing stuff like playing soccer or running in gym class," I said. "But here, we have a good team and we don't have to keep our powers secret!"

"That is very cool," Megan agreed.

We arrived at the mess hall and found Amanda waiting for us at the door. She looked pretty upset.

"What's wrong?" I asked.

"It's Sam," said Amanda. "He's gone."

"What do you mean by 'gone'?" asked Megan.

Amanda shook her head sadly. "Sam is in big trouble. He just totally destroyed Battlin' Bertram's new car. With his bare hands. Crumpled it into a little red metal ball."

"What? Why would Sam do something like that?" Megan gasped. "It must have been an accident."

Amanda shook her head. "On purpose, according to Simon, who saw the whole thing."

"That can't be right!" I exclaimed.

Amanda continued. "Simon was walking along by the parking lot when he heard all this noise—banging and crashing, the sound of metal being crushed—so he went to see what was happening and there was Sam, ripping apart Bertram's brand-new sedan. He tore off the doors and ripped off the hood and was yanking the wheels off one by one. He was in a total frenzy! Simon asked what he was doing and Sam said he was sick and tired of keeping his superpower in check and that it wasn't fair the Feds wouldn't let him use his full strength, and since

Bertram is a member of the board, he decided to get revenge."

I couldn't believe what I was hearing. It was crazy! "Where's Sam now?" I asked. "Maybe we can talk to him. . . ."

"He's gone," Amanda said again. "When Simon told him he was going to be expelled, he took off into the forest. Simon tried to catch him, but Sam kept knocking down trees and throwing boulders to block the path."

Amanda excused herself to go discuss the incident with Bertram. After she left, the three of us were silent for a long moment, letting the horrible news sink in. I just couldn't believe that Sam—or any one of my new superfriends—would do something so terrible.

"Well, I'm totally shocked," Megan said at last as we headed for the mess hall. "But I'm glad we found out what a jerk he is before the Courageous Cup began. Doesn't sound like he'd have been much of a team player."

I didn't comment. I still couldn't believe that Sam had destroyed the car on purpose. Something weird was going on.

"Now that we've lost Sam and Melanie," said Casey, "we're going to be at a real disadvantage in the contest."

"Yeah," said Megan. "All the other teams will have eight members, but we'll only have six. We won't stand a chance. And Amanda will freak if we don't win."

So will Zander, I thought.

"We should probably forfeit," said Megan.

"I agree," said Casey. "And I'm sure the boys will want to quit, too."

"Quit?" I stopped dead on the top step. "Quitting is for . . . well, quitters."

"Yeah," said Megan. "And losing is for losers."

I shook my head. "Losing is better than quitting, as long as you try."

Casey rolled her eyes. "Zoe, have you *met* our counselor? You know—Amanda, the one who gets us up at five a.m. to train because the very thought of losing makes her break out in hives? She will totally *not* be happy if we lose."

"True," I said. "Amanda will be disappointed if we lose. But I bet she'd be completely ashamed of us if we just gave up! I think we have to go through with the contest and do the best job the six of us can do."

My cabinmates considered this for a moment.

"Zoe's right," said Megan as we stepped through the doorway to the dining room. "Let's give it our best shot."

"I agree," said Casey, heading for the table we shared with the Bravery boys. "And as far as Sam is concerned, well, let's just forget all about that whole car-wrecking thing."

"Right," said Megan. "Put it clear out of our superminds."

"Uh . . . ," I said, reaching the table where our teammates were already seated, "that might not be as easy as it sounds."

Because there, sitting in the middle of our table like some crazy modern-art sculpture, sat a crumpled ball of shiny red metal.

CHAPTER 11

"**WHAT** is *that* doing there?" I demanded, glaring first at Dave, then Zander, then Howie. "I hope you guys don't think this is funny!"

"Don't blame us," said Howie. "Simon put it there."

"Why would he do that?" Megan asked.

Simon appeared at Megan's shoulder. "It's supposed to be an inspiration," he said.

"Inspiration to do what?" Casey whispered to me in a sarcastic tone. "Become drivers in a demolition derby?"

"You've heard what Sam did, right?" Simon asked.

We nodded somberly.

"I've put this nasty hunk of ruined metal here to remind you all how important teamwork is. Even though Sam let the team down, the rest of you should pull together and work hard. You shouldn't let this sort of thing discourage you."

"Why would it?" asked Zander.

"Well," said Simon in a serious tone, "I wouldn't want you to give up on the idea of teamwork just because Sam proved that you never can tell if and when a teammate might completely lose it." He gave us a sad look.

I frowned. What was Simon talking about? If this was supposed to be a pep talk, it was a pretty terrible one!

"The thing is," Simon continued, "that Sam thought his power was cooler than any of your powers." He raised his eyebrows. "The truth is that you all know which one of you has the coolest power."

He gave one last meaningful look at the squashed remains of Bertram's car, then walked away. We were silent for a moment. Finally, Casey asked the question we all wanted to ask.

"Who do you think he meant when he said we know who has the coolest power?"

I was surprised to see a small, smug smile tug at the corners of Zander's mouth. "He *was* looking at me when he said it."

Dave whirled to face at Zander. "No, he wasn't. He was looking at me."

"He sure wasn't looking at me," said Howie.

"C'mon," said Zander. "You really think stretchiness is cooler than lightning speed?"

"Well, yeah, as a matter of fact, I do."

"Puh-leez. Speed is way cooler." Zander turned to me. "Right, Zoe?"

"Don't drag her into this," snapped Dave.

"Don't tell me what to do, Taffy Boy."

"Don't call me Taffy Boy."

"Fine. How's Spandex Man grab ya?"

"Guys!" I said, holding up my hands for silence. "Knock it off!"

84

"Really," huffed Megan, putting her hands on her hips. "You sound like a couple of babies."

"Honestly," said Casey. "I mean, c'mon, you don't see us girls bickering over who has the coolest power."

"Not that there'd be any question," said Megan.

Casey slid her a look. "What's that supposed to mean? Are you saying that flying is a better power than superhearing or super-speed?"

"Flying *is* pretty awesome, you've gotta admit that."

"Well, so is superhearing."

Megan snickered. "Yeah, I'm sure that one comes in really handy. After all, you can hear the ice cream truck when it's five whole blocks away, so I guess you're always first in line."

"As a matter of fact, I am," growled Casey. "So how'd you like a toasted almond bar stuffed up your nose? Or should I say up your beak, Bird Girl?"

"Are you saying my nose looks like a beak?"

"Maybe. Or maybe I'm just calling you a birdbrain."

"I'm a flying superhero, not a bird!"

"Yeah, well, if you *were* a bird, you'd be a buzzard!"

"Girls!" I shouted.

They spun around to glare at me, but before I could say any-thing, Amanda's voice boomed, "What's going on here?"

No one answered.

"After all our talk about teamwork, this is how you behave? I'm really disappointed."

"Sorry," said Zander. "I guess the whole mess with Sam has us all feeling edgy."

"All the more reason for you guys to hang together as a team," said Amanda. "Your punishment for this unacceptable display is to clean up the entire campgrounds. You can come back here for lunch and then dinner. After dinner, you will go right back to your bunks. No swimming, no hiking, no tennis, no archery, no arts and crafts . . ."

"And no training!" said Zander. "Are you saying you aren't going to give us our afternoon workout?"

I was as surprised as Zander. Amanda seemed like the ultra-competitive type. Would she really take the risk of letting us skip practice just to teach us a lesson?

In reply, Amanda gave Zander a firm nod. "No workout," she said.

"But what about the contest? We want to win!"

"So do I," said Amanda. "But some things are even more important than winning."

"Nothing is more important than winning!" said Zander.

"Maybe that's something you should think about while you're emptying the trash cans and scrubbing down picnic tables. Think about that, and about the importance of trust and mutual respect," Amanda said as she turned and walked away.

"We're never gonna win now," said Casey. "Six kids, no practice."

"Sometimes the underdog turns out to be the champion," Howie pointed out.

"Easy for you to say," said Dave. "You *are* the underdog." He gave Howie a grin. "No offense."

We got our breakfast from the buffet and ate in silence. Later, when all the other campers were running off to enjoy a day of fun, we followed Amanda to the maintenance cabin to gather our equipment.

Ten minutes later, we were carrying trash bags, buckets, and sponges.

"Start in the east corner and work your way back here," Amanda commanded.

What else could we do? We headed east.

Cleanup duty was a total drag. And the worst part was, I didn't even deserve it.

"This isn't fair," I grumbled, picking up a crumpled candy wrapper and stuffing it into my trash bag. "I wasn't the one calling people names."

"I heard that," snapped Casey from twenty feet away.

"Well, it's true," I said.

Zander was dunking a sponge into a bucket of soapy water. "We should be training," he said, slapping the sponge onto a wooden picnic table and beginning to scrub. "How are we going to win if we're not in shape?"

As he spoke, he scrubbed faster and faster until he was cleaning at superspeed. Soapsuds lathered up and splattered all over the place.

"Jeesh," said Dave, reaching across three other picnic tables to grab the sponge out of Zander's hand. "Watch what you're doing!"

We all looked and saw that Zander had scrubbed so hard he'd completely worn through the middle plank of the picnic table.

"Oh, great," said Megan. "Now we're going to be punished for destroying camp property. Good going, Zander."

Zander stooped down and picked up an empty juice box. "So much for teamwork," he muttered.

This time, Casey didn't say "I heard that," but I was pretty sure from the snotty look she gave him that she had heard, all right.

At ten o'clock, the sun vanished and the sky darkened, and by ten-fifteen, it was pouring (this time without any superassistance from Megan and Zander). Amanda arrived with an umbrella and told us to go back to our cabins.

When we got there, rain was pelting our roof and coming in through the screens, making puddles on our windowsills.

"Well, I guess if we were gonna be stuck inside, this is the day for it," I said.

"That doesn't make me feel any better," said Casey.

"Me either," said Megan.

They were the only words we spoke to each other for the rest of morning. In the Intrepid cabin, morale had just reached an all-time superpowered low.

CHAPTER 12

AT noon, we put on our rain gear and dashed through the storm to the mess hall. I dashed at superspeed, which got me there way before my cabinmates. I found Howie standing under an umbrella and waiting for me on the front steps.

"How were things in the new Bravery cabin this morning?" I asked. The boys' group had been moved to a temporary cabin while their old one was being repaired.

"Miserable. Zander and Dave wouldn't even look at each other."

"Same thing in Intrepid."

"I used the time to do some research," said Howie. He reached into the pocket of his electric green slicker and pulled out a communication device. "It's Sam's," he explained. "He was showing me how to use it last night. Very intriguing piece of technology. Hope I get one of my own someday."

"Aww, Howie." I gave him an encouraging look. "I'm sure you will. Someday."

"Well, while Dave and Zander were giving each other the silent treatment, I connected with your pal Thatcher. Turns out he's one of Grandpa Gil's biggest fans! Anyway, I asked him to do me a favor and log on to the Internet from the communications hub. I can only imagine the computer setup they've got in that place. So I managed to do a little research on the Sweep."

"Really?"

"Yeah. It's a fascinating story. Good being sucked in by evil and all that."

"What did you find out?"

"Well, what Amanda neglected to mention is that the Sweep is still a fugitive from superjustice." He opened the door to the mess hall and held it for me as I walked inside.

"What are you saying?"

"I'm saying," said Howie, peeling off his slicker, "that the Sweep is still out there somewhere!"

Lunch was depressing. Megan and Casey arrived, followed soon after by Dave and Zander, but no one sat at our regular table. Instead, Zander and Casey took a table near the fireplace, Megan ate with the kids from the Integrity cabin, and Dave went off by himself to have his lunch while watching sitcom reruns in the rec room.

Howie and I took a table near the window that looked out over the lake.

"I found out some other stuff, too," he said, dipping his spoon into his bowl of chicken noodle soup. "The Federation thinks there's going to be another all-powered hero very soon."

"You mean another Super with every power, like the Sweep?" I wasn't sure if this was good news or bad. "What if this new one turns evil, too?"

Howie shrugged. "Highly unlikely. The Sweep had a big-time character flaw—a major ego. My guess is that when this new hero emerges, the Feds will keep a close eye on him or her to be sure he or she doesn't get too full of himself."

"Or herself." I munched a crouton from my salad. "Didn't Amanda say that a hero with every power was a once-in-an-eon thing?"

"Generally," said Howie. "I guess we're having a particularly powerful eon. Anyway, the Feds are always on the watch for the Sweep, but so far, there hasn't been any sign of him. They're hoping the new all-powered one will show up soon so they'll have someone to battle the Sweep. Hey, if you're not going to eat your cole slaw, can I have it?"

I pushed my tray toward him so he could scoop the cole slaw onto his plate. I wished the rest of the team were here, but everyone was still angry about the nasty things that had been said at breakfast. I turned to look out the window at the rain, thinking about the Sweep out there in the world, waiting to use his powers to wreak havoc.

"How about your cupcake?" Howie was saying. "Gonna eat that?"

"You can have it."

I handed Howie my dessert, then went back to staring out at the rain. The weather seemed to fit my mood—gloomy. I was confused and even a little scared and found myself wishing, just a bit, that instead of being here at Camp Courageous learning how to fight evil and protect the planet, I were somewhere far away with Emily, picking out hair ribbons and learning how to bounce soccer balls off my head.

Since we couldn't clean outdoors because of the rain, Amanda switched our punishment to indoor cleanup. Howie and I were on dish-washing duty. Casey and Zander got stuck going through the trash, searching for an orthodontic retainer one of the campers had accidentally thrown away.

"Gross," said Zander, digging under a banana peel.

Megan was flying around with a feather duster, dusting the ceiling fans, while Dave swept the entire mess hall. Lucky for him he could do it standing in one spot, just stretching his arms as they moved the broom.

Over in the rec room, we could hear the other campers having a blast playing charades.

"I hope everyone forgives and forgets by tomorrow," I said to Howie, drying my seventy-fifth plastic plate.

"Me too!" said Howie, rinsing a pile of silverware. "Otherwise, the underdogs are going to lose big-time!"

CHAPTER

13

Tuesday, Day 4, Activities and Workshops

9:00 a.m., Morning Activities (Elective)

101 Uses For Your Supermask
Come learn how to make the most of your identity-concealing mask. This standard-issue hero accessory can double as a slingshot, a first-aid bandage, and, in a real pinch, a fashionable hair bow. Also to be discussed: updating an old supersuit for today's style.
Location: Mess Hall

Arts and Crafts
Macramé, basket-weaving, and rubber-stamp projects.
Location: Rec Room

Archery
Learn to shoot flaming arrows. This activity is for fireproof heroes only.
Location: Flagpole

The next day, the Intrepid team, plus Howie, all chose Bertram's wife's arts and crafts workshop. Matilda was terrific—tiny but high-energy, with silvery blond hair and a booming voice. She looked familiar to me, and it took me a moment to remember where I'd seen her—Electra had used her as the inspiration for a character in a Lightning Girl comic once: Glue Gun Girl. She'd saved the world by hot-gluing a superbad guy to a brick wall.

"Saving the world is a wonderful pastime," Matilda told us, handing out heavy white cord for the macramé project. "But even Supers need some relaxation. Now, watch carefully."

She began to demonstrate the intricate skills involved in making a hanging plant holder. My hope was that the workshops would get my friends out of their angry moods. But even after two hours of knotting string into macramé plant holders, the dark mood of our team was lingering. Everyone—with the exception of Howie and me—was still mad about what had happened the day before.

During the arts and crafts, Howie and I attempted to make pleasant small talk. I told him all about Emily's letter and the fun she was having at soccer camp. I tried to get the others involved in the conversation, but nobody would join in. As soon as we finished with our plant hangers, Amanda hustled us outside to continue our training along with the rest of Bravery cabin.

Amanda was too focused on making up for lost training time to notice the dissension in her ranks. I was pretty sure Simon noticed, but he seemed unbothered by the team's attitude problem. In fact, he was in a pretty upbeat mood; maybe he was hoping to jolly us all of out of our gloom. If so, he'd set himself an uphill task.

"Here is the schedule of Courageous Cup events," he said.

"Wednesday: River Rapids Race. Thursday: Mountain-Climbing Challenge, and Friday: Scavenger Hunt."

"Sounds like fun," I said brightly, looking from Megan to Casey. "I've always wanted to try white-water rafting."

"Hmmpf." Megan rolled her eyes.

Casey folded her arms across her chest. "Psssht."

"I bet the view from the mountaintop will be amazing," Howie offered, grinning at Zander and Dave.

Dave frowned. Zander turned his back.

"And hey," I said, forcing a cheery tone, "who doesn't love a good old-fashioned scavenger hunt?"

Nobody answered.

Amanda gave a loud blast on her whistle, and everyone dropped to the ground to do push-ups.

We spent the rest of the day training in silence.

Before sunrise on Wednesday, I heard a gentle tapping on the screen door. I looked across the cabin to see if Casey had tuned in, but she was still sound asleep. I guess she'd shifted out of superhearing mode to get a good night's sleep before the cup contest.

Quietly, I climbed down from my bunk and opened the cabin door.

Howie was sitting on the front stoop, his chin in his hand.

"Sorry to wake you," he whispered.

"Nah." I shook my head. "I was already awake. I've been up worrying for hours." I sat down next to Howie.

"Think we stand a chance today?" he asked.

I shrugged. "Not if the team doesn't have a major attitude adjustment before the challenges begin. And it doesn't look like that's gonna happen. Megan and Casey ignored each other all through dinner last night, and when we got back to the cabin, I couldn't stand the silence, so I suggested we play a game of cards."

"Did they agree to play?"

"Yeah." I frowned. "But only if we played War."

"Ah. And how did that go?"

"I should have stuck with the silence."

Howie let out a long rush of breath. "I would have liked to be on the winning team. Not for me, you understand. But for my grandpa Gil. I mean, I've been here four days and there's still no sign of me turning super. At least I could have made him proud of me by winning a trophy."

"I'm sure your grandpa is already proud of you," I said.

Howie nodded. "I know. But . . ."

His voice trailed off. We sat for a while, listening to the last chirps of the crickets as the sun rose in a pale shimmer of pink and gold beyond the lake.

I wanted to tell Howie that I was proud of him. I wanted to say that even if he never got his powers, he'd always be a winner in my book, just for being smart and kind, and fun, in his quirky way. Just for being Howie.

But it was one of those moments when it seemed better just to share the silence.

Besides, even if I didn't say those things to Howie, deep down, I think he probably already knew.

At nine a.m. sharp, the entire camp gathered at the flagpole for opening ceremonies. Music blared through the PA system as Bertram stood on the highest step of the main lodge, holding the huge unlit torch.

"And now, with the ceremonial lighting of the torch," he announced, "the Courageous Cup contest will officially commence."

One of the counselors joined Bertram on the step and rather unceremoniously proceeded to light the giant torch with an ordinary wooden match. I felt a pang of sadness, knowing how much Melanie had been looking forward to igniting the flame that would begin the contest. I glanced at my teammates; I had a hunch they were feeling the same way.

Once the torch was blazing, Bertram held it up high and the whole camp cheered.

The Courageous Cup contest was under way.

Amanda led us down a wooded path we hadn't seen before. Simon brought up the rear, making sure no one got lost or left behind.

I caught up to Amanda. "I was wondering," I began in a whisper, "what happened to Sam? I mean, I know he took off, but is anyone searching for him?"

Amanda shrugged. "Bertram isn't saying much about it except that the Federation has put an all points bulletin out on him."

"Do you think he'll come back to camp?" I asked. I felt a

twinge of fear. As hard as it was to believe, I had to allow for the fact that Sam might have gone over to the dark side, and he might be lurking in the woods right now. I guess what Howie had said about the Sweep's being on the loose was making me jumpy.

"Doubtful. He knows he'll be captured if he does."

But how do you capture someone who's stronger than superstrong? I wondered.

The path ended at the river. The bank sloped steeply down to the water, which was rough from the previous day's rain. The rapids swirled and foamed over the large rocks jutting out from the shallower spots. A few yards away, several inflatable yellow rafts were set out along the bank. I could see the one with the Intrepid/Bravery flag attached.

"Our first event is the white-water river race," Amanda said, consulting the contest program. "We'll be competing against Team Integrity/Fortitude. The object of the race is to navigate the rapids and be the first team to cross the finish line, which is two miles downriver."

Simon pulled a large rolled-up piece of paper from his backpack and handed it to Amanda.

"This map charts the river," she told us. "It will tell you where the stronger rapids are, where the water is deepest, where the tributaries branch off, and so on. You will study this map as a team. Knowing what to expect is the best way to stay in control on your raft." She handed the map to me, then turned to Simon. "Come with me, please," she said. "I want to do a safety check on our raft before we begin."

I sat down on the ground and unrolled the map. Howie crouched beside me.

"Gather around, everyone, let's have a look," I said.

Nobody budged.

"That's it!" Howie snapped. "I've had it!"

His shout startled me; it startled all of us. He was scowling at our four teammates. "Yesterday we were all upset about Sam, and some of us said some things we didn't mean. But c'mon! We're superheroes. Well, you guys are, and I sure hope I'll be one soon. I know that Supers stand up for what is right and just in the world! They're supposed to be forces of good, but how can you be an example of goodness if you can't even forgive your own friends? Now I want all of you to stop acting like morons and start acting like teammates. Superteammates. Got it?"

For a moment there was absolute silence. Suddenly, Zander grinned his crooked grin. "You know something? He's right . . . again."

I let out a huge sigh of relief as the four of them shook hands and apologized. I gave Howie a high five. Then they all gathered around the map and we studied it together.

Zander pointed to the spot that showed the most powerful rapids. "We'll have to look out for this one," he said. "And here . . . it drops off pretty quickly. That's the deepest point in the whole river."

"And it occurs at the widest spot," Casey observed.

"There seem to be some pretty nasty rock formations over here," said Dave.

"We'll have to look out for those," said Megan.

Amanda and Simon came back, carrying our raft. Inside it were six life jackets.

"Who's ready for a little ride?" asked Simon.

The Integrity/Fortitude team arrived with their counselors. We all shook hands and wished each other luck, then put on our life vests and climbed into our rafts.

"On your mark, get set . . . go!"

Zander shoved us off from the bank and jumped into the raft.

The power of the river was amazing; right away I could feel the strength of the current pulling us along, with the Integrity/Fortitude team right beside us.

"Paddle!" cried Zander. "Now, lean left, everyone. . . ."

We leaned together, guiding the raft with our weight. The oars slapped the surface in perfect rhythm, splashing cool, clean water. We were moving quickly, pulling ahead of the other raft.

"We've got the lead!" cried Dave. "We're leaving them in the dust."

I looked behind us and saw the Integrity/Fortitude raft lagging. They couldn't seem to get their paddling in sync. One of the girls wasn't even bothering to paddle; she was reapplying her lip gloss while two of the boys argued over which of them got to sit next to her.

Teamwork, I thought. *That's why we're winning!*

Suddenly, Howie was pointing ahead, where the river flowed through a narrow gully. The water swelled and parted in the center, revealing jagged dark shapes just below the surface. "Hey, guys, I don't remember those rocks on the map."

"Neither do I," said Megan.

"Well, at least they're in a calm spot," observed Dave. "We should be able to paddle our way around them."

Just as he said it, though, the water around the rocks began to roil. Waves kicked up and tumbled furiously, worse than any of the rapids we'd seen so far. As we floated toward them, they became more violent. The noise they made was nearly deafening.

"Does anyone hear that?" asked Casey.

"All I hear are the waves," I shouted. "What do you hear?"

"Air. Hissing. You know, like a leak. In a raft."

Sure enough, the raft was deflating . . . and fast. The rounded sides were wrinkling and shrinking as the air poured out of them. Water began to spill in.

"We have to abandon ship!" cried Casey.

"Do we have to?" Megan looked nervous. "I know I'm super, but I've never been crazy about deep water!"

I knew how she felt. Even a superhero wearing a life vest could swallow too much water and choke. And what about Howie? He wouldn't be able to keep his head above water in a current like this.

"Howie," I shouted, "is your life vest buckled tight? You're going to have to swim! Stay close to me and I'll help you."

"I have a better idea," yelled Howie. "Dave, stretch yourself toward the bank, and we can all grab on to you."

Dave immediately reached out with both arms and wrapped them around a sturdy tree on the riverbank. We all took hold of him and clung like crazy. The shriveling raft bobbed on the rough surface for only a moment before sinking into the depths of the wild water. A giant wave crashed over us; the force of it almost knocked Howie off Dave, but Megan grabbed Howie's life vest just in time.

Dave retracted his arms without letting go of the tree and pulled us onto the bank. Now we were all soaking and cold, but at least we were safe.

Amanda ran up a few moments later. She looked confused and worried. "I saw what happened," she said. "What went wrong?"

"I don't know," said Zander. "One minute everything was going great, and the next it was chaos. What I don't understand is why those rocks weren't on the map."

"Or why our raft deflated," I added, looking at Amanda. "You and Simon just checked it."

Simon came running out of the woods. He was dripping wet and he looked terribly worried. "I was downriver waiting for you when I saw your paddles come drifting past. What happened?"

Amanda explained it all to Simon. He was quiet for a moment, thinking.

"As far as I know," he said, "no team has ever used their powers during a cup challenge before. I don't know what the rules are, but I'm afraid you may be disqualified from the entire contest because Dave used his power."

Dave seemed ready to squirm, and his face went bright red.

"I used my power, too," Casey said quickly. "I heard the raft leaking with my superhearing. So don't blame Dave."

"Yeah, don't blame Dave," said Zander.

"If it hadn't been for Dave," I said, "we all could have drowned! Howie especially, because he doesn't have any powers that might have saved him."

"Did I sound as though I was blaming him?" said Simon, looking apologetic. "I didn't mean to." He patted Dave on the shoulder. "Good work, Dave. Really." Then he gave Howie a big smile. "Would have hated to see you go under, Howie. I mean that. But still, rules are rules."

"Hey, look," said Zander, pointing back toward the river.

We all turned to see the Integrity/Fortitude team drifting past in their raft. Oddly, the swell of white water that had nearly taken us under had stopped and the current in that spot was calm, just like the map had indicated.

The girl who'd been putting on lip gloss was now touching up her eye shadow, and the rest of the team was still trying to get the hang of paddling.

"Ah," said Simon. "And there go the winners of the raft race."

"That is *so* not fair!" said Casey. "We were the better team."

"It's okay, guys," said Amanda. "Keep your spirits up. We've still got two more events."

"If we're not disqualified," Dave muttered. "'Cause of me."

"Not because of you," said Howie. "Because of me. You used

your power to save me. I'm sure Bertram won't disqualify you for that. You are a superhero, after all. That's part of your job description."

"I think Howie's right," said Amanda. "I'll talk to Bertram. He'll see that Dave didn't have a choice."

She took one last disappointed glance at the shriveled remains of the raft, now draped limply on the far bank, and headed back to camp.

When she was gone, Simon gave us a sympathetic look. "Don't feel too bad about losing the raft race," he said. "I suppose knowing when you're beaten could be considered an admirable quality. You did your best. At least, I think you did."

"What's that supposed to mean?" demanded Zander.

"Nothing, except that . . . well, I would have liked to see you make more of an effort to keep going."

I considered his remark. Maybe he had a point . . . sort of. We hadn't even tried to come up with a way to stay afloat and make it to the finish line. Howie's voice interrupted my thoughts.

"How did you get all wet?" he was asking Simon.

"When I was reaching toward the water to fish out the paddles, I tumbled in."

"Where are the paddles?" Howie asked.

"I must have dropped them on my way through the woods, in my hurry to get back here and see how you all managed to mess up so badly." There was a sudden sharp glitter in Simon's eyes, as though he resented Howie's questions. "Now let's go back to camp and get you guys dried off"—he glared at Howie—"before those of you who aren't super and nearly indestructible catch a cold."

We trooped back to camp without a word.

CHAPTER

14

THE good news was that Bertram understood and ruled that the Intrepid/Bravery team would not be disqualified.

The bad news was that, for Howie's own safety, he would not be allowed to participate in the Mountain-Climbing Challenge.

Amanda broke it to us Thursday morning, just before it was time to start the second event.

"But Howie's part of the team!" said Zander.

"He's been training as hard as the rest of us," Dave added.

"I'll say it again," huffed Casey. "*So* not fair!"

Howie looked touched by the show of support. "Thanks, guys, but I understand where Bertram's coming from. Besides, I'd only slow you down, and because of yesterday's mishap, we've got to come from behind if we're going to place. I want you go out there and win this one."

"Are you sure, Howie?" I asked.

"Positive."

"Can Howie at least come along to cheer us on?" said Megan.

"Of course," said Amanda, smiling. "I wouldn't have it any other way.

"Mount Valor," Amanda announced, when we reached the base of the mountain. It was impossibly steep, and it was definitely a long way to the top. I looked up at the sparse patches of trees, the scraggly brush, the occasional outcropping of rock.

"Be right back," said Amanda. She went over to talk to the counselor of the Fearless/Energized team, who would be our competition for this task, leaving us with Simon, who was handing out our climbing equipment. I couldn't take my eyes off the mountain.

"We're supposed to climb that?" I said. "Without powers?"

"Oh, it's just a relaxing little hike," said Simon.

"I'd rather fly to the top," said Megan.

"Ah, but you can't, now, can you?" Simon shook his head. "Those are the rules. No powers. Just teamwork. Because if it were about using your powers, well, Zander would be the winner, of course. He *is* the fastest kid on earth."

I cleared my throat loudly. It wasn't that I cared if Zander was faster than me—at least, I didn't think I cared—I just didn't like being overlooked.

"Something wrong, Zoe?" Then, as if he'd suddenly remembered, Simon smacked his forehead. "Oh, that's right! You have that speedy thing going for you as well. Hmmm, then maybe *you* would be the winner."

Out of the corner of my eye, I saw Zander frown.

Simon shrugged. "Too bad our little race didn't work out the other day. Then we'd know for sure. But no matter. We're all in this together, right? Now, what was I saying? Ah, yes . . . team-work."

"Teamwork," said Howie. "And trigonometry."

"Trigonometry?" said Dave. "You mean like in school?" He made a face. "C'mon, this is summer vacation. Let's not talk about trig."

"I agree," Simon said briskly. "Save that for the classroom. Now you all get ready for the climb. I'm going to grab some water bottles for you to have if—I mean *when* you finish."

When Simon was gone, we all turned to Howie.

"What about trigonometry, Howie?" said Casey.

"Well, I'm guessing the Fearless/Energized team is going to climb straight up, going vertically toward the peak."

"And that would be wrong because . . . ?" I asked, confused. I'd never been as good as Howie in math.

"Because going straight up an incline this steep is going to require not only great balance but incredible strength, which all of you have but can't use. You'll tire yourselves out before you're halfway up. See, it's all about angle measurement and tangents, but I don't want to bore you with all that."

"I'm grateful," said Megan.

"I can sum it up in one word," said Howie. "And that word is simple: *zigzag*."

"Huh?" said Dave.

"I think I understand," I said. "Instead of climbing straight up, Howie wants us to zigzag our way to the top. First we go up sort of sideways in one direction, which will make the climb less steep; then still go up, but sideways in the other direction."

"By creating an angular path, you'll conserve energy and experience better balance," Howie concluded.

"Trigonometry," said Zander. "Who knew?"

"Howie knew," I said, laughing.

Dave gave Howie a high five. "Zigzag!"

"Go for it!" said Howie.

"What about you?" asked Megan.

Howie sat down beneath a big tree and pulled out Sam's forgotten communication device. "I'll be waiting here, chatting with Thatcher," he said.

Using Howie's zigzag strategy, we made our way up the mountain. We could see the Fearless/Energized team heading straight for the top, just as Howie predicted.

"They're farther along than we are," Zander observed, sounding a little worried.

"But they'll be exhausted before they reach the midway point," I assured him. "And we'll still be going strong."

We worked together, pointing out footholds to one another, and warning our teammates where the ground turned slippery.

Sure enough, halfway to the peak, we'd caught up to the other team. We could tell they were losing steam. Even without super-hearing, I could hear Sunny complaining about how thirsty she was.

"She looks pretty beat," said Zander.

"You should go offer to help her," I teased. "Maybe she's got a bottle of water you can open for her."

As Zander and I joked, a small stone came rolling past. Then another. Then another, larger rock came thumping by.

"I don't like the look of that," I said.

Dave shaded his eyes and looked toward the top of the mountain. "Uh-oh."

We all looked. A giant boulder was rocking back and forth, throwing off smaller stones as it came loose from the mountainside. Slowly, it began to skid downward. And we were directly in its path.

"Quick," cried Zander. "Get out of the way!"

"Why bother?" asked Casey. "If we go into Super mode, we'll be fine. That boulder could roll right over us, and we wouldn't even feel it."

"Yeah," Zander replied, "but if we don't go into Super mode, we can stay in the contest."

"Good point," said Dave.

"But what about Howie?" I asked. "He's at the bottom of the mountain. That boulder is headed right toward him."

The urgency of the situation hit us all at once. Our friend Howie was in danger—again!

"Contest or no contest, we have to stop that boulder!" said Megan. "I don't care if we get disqualified. I don't want Howie to get crushed!"

"Me either!" said Zander, looking up toward the giant rock as it continued to tumble down. "Okay, so what's the plan?"

"Catch it?" Dave suggested.

"We can redirect it," I said. "Remember my letter from Emily?"

Megan and Casey caught on at the same time. "Yes!" cried Casey.

"Time for a game of soccer," said Megan.

"Supersoccer," Casey corrected her.

We all went into Super mode, hooking into our strength just in time as we positioned ourselves in the formation Emily had described in her letter. The boulder came bounding down toward us, casting its shadow like a dark cloud.

It reached Casey first; she kicked her leg out as hard as she could, propelling the rock toward Megan, who leaped upward and used a bicycle kick to shoot it to me.

Closing my eyes tight, I leaned into the boulder and let it bounce off my head, sending it sideways in the opposite direction from the Fearless/Energized team, and far from where we'd left Howie under the tree. The giant rock sailed away in a wide arc, then slammed to the ground to continue its journey down the mountainside toward a dense area of forest, where we were sure no other campers would be caught unaware.

We all looked and saw that our rivals had continued on their way. . . using the zigzag strategy and making great time.

"They copied us!" huffed Casey.

"We lose again," Dave muttered.

Strangely, Zander didn't seem to care that we had no hope of winning the mountain climb. "First the unexpected rapids, now a boulder," he said. "This is getting *very* weird."

We made our way down the mountain to where Simon was waiting in the shade with Howie.

"Back so soon?" Simon asked.

"Yeah," said Zander. "The road got a little rocky. Literally."

Megan explained about the giant rock.

Simon made a *tsk-tsk* sound with his tongue. "Tough break, kids. You must be getting awfully discouraged."

I looked around at my teammates and realized he was right. "Um, Zander, can I talk to you for a moment? I think we need a quick cocaptains' meeting."

Zander followed me away from the others. He looked miserable.

"Morale is pretty low," I said.

"Well, what do you expect?" he grumbled. "First we lose Mel, then Sam goes wonky, then the raft disaster, and now this. I really thought we had a chance to win this cup, but now I don't think there's any way we can pull it off." He kicked at a stone on the ground. "I must be a pretty crummy captain if I can't lead my team through these challenges without failing on every count."

I couldn't believe my ears. "Zander," I said, "first, you are not the only captain of this team. So if you've failed, then so have I." I didn't wait for him to reply. "And second, there's no way all these things could be coincidence. I think someone is sabotaging us."

"What do you mean?"

"Let's go back to the beginning. We don't know for sure that Mel caused that fire—it could have been someone with a match, not fire-starting superpowers. And as far as Sam is concerned, I'm having a hard time believing he vandalized Bertram's car because he was angry about being on restricted power—he seemed fine with it to me. He wasn't harboring a grudge against the Feds."

"So what do you think happened?"

"Well, Simon said Sam was out of control, right? Maybe

113

somebody got to him and . . . I don't know, *made* him rip Bertram's car to pieces. Maybe he was hypnotized or something, and that's why he told Simon all that stuff about being angry."

"I guess it's possible," said Zander. "And if you believe in that theory, it's not so hard to imagine that someone could have deliberately weakened our raft and made that rock fall. Whew, someone must want us out of this competition really badly." He looked very solemn. "Maybe there's a villain hiding out under-cover at Camp Courageous after all."

It was a terrible thought, but I found myself hoping it was true . . . because the only other possibility was much, much worse. If it wasn't an undercover villain causing the trouble . . . it was one of the superkids.

CHAPTER

15

I was jumpy the whole rest of the day. I studied every camper, looking for suspicious behavior, but everyone seemed normal. Well, normal for superkids, at least. By dinner I was exhausted from worrying.

During dessert, Bertram stood up at the front of the mess hall and called for our attention. "As you know, tomorrow we finish our Courageous Cup contest with the traditional scavenger hunt. Each team will be given a list of different items to be found and collected."

He held up a sealed envelope. "The lists are in here; no one besides me has seen them. Not even your counselors know what you'll be looking for. Each item is described in a riddle, so you'll have to first figure out what the item is and then hunt it down. You will have two hours to collect the items. I wish you all the best of luck! And don't forget . . . no superpowers."

When we left the dining hall, the Intrepid/Bravery team met

on the shore of the lake. Fireflies twinkled in the dusk, and the lapping of the water on the sand was like a peaceful song.

"Listen up, team," said Zander. "Zoe and I were talking this afternoon, and we're afraid that there's been some foul play."

"What do you mean?" asked Megan.

"We think someone tampered with the raft," I said. "And that boulder—we think it was pushed."

"Someone's out to get us?" said Dave.

Zander nodded.

"I don't understand," said Casey. "We're super. We couldn't have been hurt by the leaky raft or the rolling boulder, so what was the point?"

"We don't think they wanted to hurt us," I said. "We think they were trying to psych us out. Maybe even get us to drop out of the contest."

"I felt like dropping out after Sam took off," Megan admitted.

"After the boulder, I was ready to quit," Dave confessed.

"We think that's exactly what this person is trying to do," said Zander.

"What difference does it make if we drop out of the contest?" Casey asked. "There's still plenty of competition from the other teams. Why target us?"

"Because," said Howie, "you guys are amazing! And somebody out there is just plain jealous."

"Thanks, Howie," I said, feeling my cheeks grow warm. "But everybody at Camp Courageous is exceptional."

"Don't you get it?" he persisted. "At a camp full of exceptional kids, you're the most exceptional of all! You guys have the coolest superpowers of anyone at Camp Courageous. But there's more to this team than its powers."

"Our dazzling good looks?" Dave teased.

"You guys work together," Howie said, still serious. "You train harder than any other team in this camp and you don't complain. And when you found out I was the only kid at this camp without powers, you didn't try to dump me. You accepted me—even better, you treated me like a friend. When I had something to say, you listened. When I was in danger, you looked out for me."

I heard a sniffle and glanced over at Casey. She was wiping a tear from the corner of her eye. I didn't blame her. Howie's speech was making me feel a little choked up, too.

"I know we almost blew the whole teamwork thing by getting angry with each other, but we even managed to work that out. See? Powers are great, but there's one thing in this world that no one—super or otherwise—can beat. And that's friendship. So I say we go out there tomorrow not just as a team, but as best friends . . . and do our best."

"And work together," said Casey.

"And have fun!" I added.

"And win," said Zander. As soon as he said it, he snapped his mouth shut. Even in the dim light I could see him blushing. "Um, I mean . . ."

"Aw, what the heck," I said, laughing. "Let's have fun *and* win!"

The air seemed charged with excitement the next morning when all the teams gathered at the center of camp to receive our lists for the scavenger hunt. Each team would be given four items to collect. The first team to retrieve all four would be the winner.

Bertram called the counselors up and handed them a folded piece of paper, which they brought back to their teams.

As we were waiting for the signal to read our lists, Simon pulled me aside.

"Watch out for Zander," he said in a low voice. "He's a glory hound. He'll try to steal the show."

Before I could reply, he'd skittered away and started whispering something to Dave.

I hoped it was something more positive than what he'd said to me. I was beginning to think Simon was not the best counselor in the world—he sure didn't know the meaning of the words *pep talk*!

"On the count of three," Bertram's voice boomed, "teams, read your lists. One . . . two . . . *three!*"

Amanda opened the folded sheet and we all leaned in to see.

Read the clues to determine the treasures you must seek. The first team to retrieve all four treasures and bring them to the main lodge is the winner.

1. I stand for you, you stand for me.
   Sometimes I'm taut, and then I go slack.
   Grounded is something I never should be.
   When I wave at you, you needn't wave back.

2. Here's your second clue, so don't blow it:
   Bertram likes to hang around with me because I'm a real blast.

3. You will find me at 30° latitude/90° longitude.

4. I am symbolic of victory, and my symbol is Ag.

Amanda read the first riddle aloud.

"It's rude not to wave back at someone who waves to you," said Casey.

I giggled. "It's not rude if the someone waving to you is a flag," I said.

We all looked to the top of the flagpole, where our camp banner was snapping proudly beneath Old Glory.

"That's the answer," said Dave. "The first item is a flag. But which one?"

"Not the camp flag," said Howie. "Look at the clue. The American flag can never be allowed to touch the ground. 'Grounded is something I never should be.' And you stand up when you pledge allegiance to it."

In the next second, Zander had run—at normal speed—to the flagpole, lowered the flag, and carefully removed it from its rope. He and Dave folded it without letting it touch the ground.

"One down," said Howie. "Three to go."

We studied the rest of the clues on the page.

"Whoa," said Megan, "these are pretty tough."

I looked around at the other teams, struggling with the riddles. So many people talking at once, so many clues and interpretations—there had to be a better strategy.

"I think we should split into pairs," I suggested. "Each pair can take one riddle and just focus on that."

Zander glared at me. "Zoe, you can't just start making up rules."

I remembered what Simon had said about Zander wanting to hog all the credit. "It's not a rule," I snapped. "It's a suggestion!"

"A good suggestion," said Howie. "Let's try it. Megan, you and Dave take the second clue. Zander, you and Casey can work on the third one. Zoe and I will take the fourth." He took the page from Amanda and tore it into three pieces, then gave each pair their assigned riddle.

"I'll hold on to the flag for you," said Amanda. "As you find the items, bring them back here to me. And Simon . . ." She turned to tell him what he could do to help.

But Simon was nowhere to be found.

"He's probably helping Bertram with something," Amanda guessed. "Now, you guys, get moving!"

Howie and I took our clue and sat down at a picnic table.

"'A symbol of victory,'" I read, then frowned. "A medal? A blue ribbon? Some sort of prize?"

"I think you're on the right track," said Howie.

"But they won't be handing out the prizes until Saturday. So I don't see that there will be any medals lying around yet."

"Let's try the second half," said Howie. "'My symbol is Ag.'" He smiled. "Gee, could it really be that simple?"

"Doesn't sound simple to me," I confessed.

"Ag is the symbol for silver on the periodic table."

Since I didn't know half as much about science as Howie did, I was willing to take his word for it. My stomach fluttered excitedly. "A silver symbol of victory . . . the Courageous Cup. The *actual* cup. The trophy!"

Howie and I looked at each other, smiled, then bolted for the main lodge.

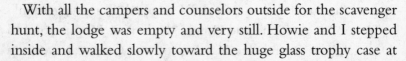

With all the campers and counselors outside for the scavenger hunt, the lodge was empty and very still. Howie and I stepped inside and walked slowly toward the huge glass trophy case at the back of the lobby. There on the top shelf sat a large silver loving cup—the very cup won by my grandpa Zack and his teammates.

Howie stood on tiptoe and read the inscription. "'This cup is awarded to the most magnificent team ever to participate in the Courageous Cup.'"

"Their names are on it," I said.

Howie kept reading. "'Zack Richards—Zip, Zeb Richards—Zeal, Battlin' Bertram Billings, and . . . and . . .'" I heard his breath catch. "'Gil "The Hunter" Hunt.'"

"Howie, your grandfather was on that team, too!"

Smiling, Howie opened the glass doors of the trophy case and reached up for the silver cup.

"Help!"

I froze. Was that someone's voice I just heard? At least, I thought it was a voice—it was such a tiny squeak, I could barely make it out. "Someone's calling for help," I said. "But where are they?"

"Help!"

"They're in here," said Howie, his tone half amazed, half horrified.

"In *where*?"

"In the cup." He looked inside, then tilted the cup so I could see. Sitting in the shiny silver bowl of the cup was our missing teammate, Sam.

CHAPTER 16

"SAM!" I screamed.

"Get me out of here!"

His little bitty voice echoed inside the silver cup.

Howie reached in and let Sam—who was about the size of a pickle—climb into his palm. Sam wrapped his arms around Howie's thumb and Howie carefully lifted him out.

"What happened?" asked Howie. "How did you get so small?"

"I got shrunk," said Sam. *"Duh."*

"But how?"

"Simon did it," said Sam. *"He took me to the parking lot and he froze me with his breath, and while I stood there like a giant icicle, he tore apart Bertram's car. Then he thawed me out and looked at me in this weird way and the next thing I knew, I was miniature! He brought me here and dropped me in this stupid cup, and that's where I've been for the last two days. I thought I'd be in there until the awards ceremony on Sunday!"* He turned his tiny face up to mine. *"Got anything to eat? I'm starving!"*

"Sorry, I don't."

"Zoe," said Howie in a strangled voice. "Think about what Sam just said. There's only been one Super who could freeze *and* shrink people . . . the Sweep!"

I stared at him in astonishment. "But . . . but that means *Simon* is the Sweep! He was supposed to be our coach! Why would he try to sabotage us?"

"I don't know, but we've got to tell the others," said Howie. "They could be in trouble! Zoe, you go on ahead at superspeed. I'll bring Sam."

I was out the door before he even finished talking.

"Going somewhere, Zoe?"

The familiar English-accented voice called out to me just as I was rounding the side of the main lodge; I skidded to a halt and came face to face with Simon. There was a cold glint in his eyes. In the distance I could hear the sounds of the scavenger hunters working on their riddles. Here in the shadow of the lodge, Simon and I couldn't be seen.

"We know all about you, Simon," I said, forcing myself to sound courageous. "Or should I say Sweep?"

"So you solved the little mystery, then?" He laughed; it was a cruel sound. "It was all so easy. You campers with your obsessive teamwork . . . and yet I planned this out all by myself. I set fire to that cabin with my own eyes, and then made Melanie think she did it by mistake."

"So the boulder and the rapids were your doing, too?" I asked, feeling the anger ignite in me.

"I can hold my breath for hours," he boasted. "I dove into the river, and when your raft approached, I used my super-strength to churn up a major rapid. The rocks were a piece of cake with my incredible strength. I just moved them from where the map said they were to where you wouldn't expect them." He laughed. "Oh, and that sneezing attack of yours during the trust fall? When everyone was looking at you and Howie, I blew that dandelion fluff directly at your nose. That little gag might have been my favorite. It wasn't super, but it was very resourceful."

I glared at him. "You wanted me to drop Howie, even though you knew he wasn't super. He would have gotten hurt!"

The Sweep rolled his eyes. "Hel-*lo* . . . That was the point!"

"What about Sam?"

"Also simple. My freezing breath caught him by surprise, so his strength was no use to him. When I shrank him, his powers shrank, too. If I'd known Bertram would choose his stupid trophy as one of the items for the hunt, I'd never have hidden Sam in there. Ah, well, too late now. But I'll be long gone before anyone knows any of this, since I'll be escaping with the power of superspeed."

"You don't have superspeed, Sweep," I reminded him.

"No . . ." He reached out and grabbed my arm. "But you do!"

I tried to break free, but he was too strong.

"You're going to piggyback me out of here at top speed!" Simon commanded. "I wish it had been Zander who happened along, though."

"You still think he's faster than me?" I asked.

Simon laughed. "I don't know. I do think if I'd taken him, I might have had a chance to sway him over to the side of evil."

"Zander would never do that!"

"Maybe not," Simon conceded. "I did my best to come between you two. You see, you were the whole reason I formed this plan to begin with."

"Zander and me?"

"Yes. Everyone thinks the Federation are holding out for another all-powered hero, like me"—EXCEPT YOU DON'T HAVE SUPERSPEED, I wanted to remind him—"but they've actually picked out you guys as the Next Best Thing. There are two of you, and you're of the same line! So apparently working together will magnify your powers!" He gave a snort. "There's that sickening teamwork concept again. The best get better when they team up, so they keep telling me. . . . Well, I was the best and the brightest of my day, so I wanted to bring you down the way they brought me down. I wanted to show you how it felt to fail—and to prove that nothing can be as good as a single all-powered hero."

I was about to tell him that everyone failed at some point in their life; the important thing was learning how to deal with it and move on. But I didn't get a chance. Because all of a sudden, Howie was there.

Howie. Totally *un*super Howie. Standing there holding a big silver trophy, scowling at the most powerful villain in the history of the world as if he were nothing more than a playground bully.

CHAPTER 17

"HOWIE," I said, "go get help!"

"Oh, please," said Simon. "Don't you get it? No one can help you against me!"

"No *one* maybe," came a voice. "But what about a whole team?"

I craned my neck and saw Zander, Dave, Casey, and Megan stepping around the side of the cabin.

"Fine," said Simon, dragging a hand through his hair and sounding thoroughly bored. "Give it your best shot."

"I can't believe we ever thought you were cute!" said Megan.

"I've got him," Dave yelled; he reached out his arms and wrapped them around and around Simon like a rope. "All I have to do is squeeze. . . ."

Simon rolled his eyes. "You're kidding, right?" He puffed up his cheeks and blew out a long, frosty breath on Dave's arms.

"He froze me!" Dave yelped, staring in horror at his arms, which had turned a disturbing shade of blue. "Now I can't squeeze."

Simon wriggled out of Dave's frozen arms—they fell to the ground and Dave started shaking them to try to retract them—and gave us an evil grin. "What else ya got?" He looked at Megan. "Maybe you should fly me around and see if I get queasy?" He laughed. "Although I've been flying for years and I haven't gotten sick yet."

"He's right," said Howie. "There's nothing we can do to him."

I whirled to face Howie. "What? How can you say that?"

"It's true," said Howie, still clutching the big, shiny silver cup. "He's the super-est of all. I mean, you and Zander may be way faster than he is . . ."

Simon snarled. "You had to bring *that* up, didn't you?"

". . . but he's got too many other powers. For example, he could . . . oh, I don't know, just shrink us with his eyes, like he did to Sam."

"Howie, shhh!" said Zander. "Don't give him any ideas."

"Well, he could," said Howie. "He could just shoot those shrinking rays out of his eyes and miniaturize each of us, one at a time."

"Excellent!" Simon let out a wicked cackle of laughter. "I'll admit, I hadn't thought of that, but it's a wonderful plan. And I think I'll start with you, Howie."

"Well," Howie said calmly, "if you must, you must."

I watched in horror as Simon narrowed his eyes and sent two brilliant red rays shooting in Howie's direction.

"Gotcha!" cried Howie, holding up the silver cup to shield himself.

The rays hit the metal cup, which acted like a mirror, reflecting the beams right back at Simon.

"No!" screamed Simon. "No!"

But he was already growing smaller and smaller. In seconds,

Simon was shivering on the ground like a little shaggy blond chipmunk.

"Howie," I cried, running over to him. "That was amazing!"

Howie bent to pick up the tiny counselor, then looked into the cup, where mini-Sam was peering up at him.

"Sam," said Howie, "have you ever heard the expression 'pick on somebody your own size'?"

Sam let out a tiny laugh. "Sure."

"Now's your chance," said Howie, sliding Simon into the cup.

We all leaned in to watch as Sam made a little bitty *L* with his finger and thumb and pressed the *L* to his forehead. "Looooo-ser!"

CAMP COURAGEOUS

Dear Melanie,
    Camp Courageous hasn't been the same without you. First of all, don't feel bad about setting the cabin on fire, because it wasn't you, it was Simon!

CAMP COURAGEOUS

Simon turned out to be the Sweep–yes way!–and he tried to sabotage us during the contest by making our raft sink and then almost causing an avalanche. He nearly escaped, taking me as a superhostage, but Howie came to the rescue. We'll fill you in on everything when we see you again. In the meantime, I've got to get some shut-eye. These last two days have been fun but tiring. By the

way, guess who won the
mountain-climbing
challenge! Fearless and
Energized! We think the
Fearless girls were just
trying to impress Zander.

Your friend,
Kid Zoom

It was Friday night. I was lying on my bunk, reading the letter I'd just finished writing to Melanie out loud to my cabinmates.

"You forgot to tell her the part about Howie shrinking Simon," said Megan.

"And Sam putting Simon in a headlock until he promised never to do anything like this again. If he ever makes it back to full size, that is." Which was looking unlikely, since Director Bertram seemed more than happy to keep Simon in the trophy cupboard until he could hand him over to the Federation. At least one of the other kids at camp had the eye-shrink thing going on and had been able to restore Sam to full size.

"And you forgot to tell her that Howie and I have a date to go canoeing tomorrow before the awards ceremony," said Casey, giggling.

"And that Zander is your cousin," said Megan.

I laughed, scribbling the additional news in a PS.

"Tell her about the soccer play we learned from Emily."

"Tell her Sam still hasn't finished his sister's change purse!"

"Tell her Dave is gonna teach me to do a backflip off the raft."

I was writing as fast as I could . . . superfast! In fact, I was writing so fast that my pen began to throw off sparks; the next second, the paper I was writing on went up in flames!

"Yikes!" I cried.

Casey hopped up, grabbed a blanket, and put out the fire.

"Well," I said, brushing the ashes off my hands, "I guess it would be better just to call her on the communication device and tell her the whole crazy story."

"Yeah," said Megan. "Of course, we'll never be able to tell anyone else."

"It's been great having you guys to talk to," I said. "And being able to use powers without worrying about getting caught. It's gonna be weird going back home and having to keep it all a secret again."

But deep down, I couldn't wait to get home. I missed my parents and my friends, and even though I hadn't had a chance to think about him for a whole week, I was really excited to see Josh Devlin, who'd be back from baseball camp—probably with a great tan.

Across the cabin, Megan yawned loudly.

"We'd better get some sleep," said Casey. "The awards ceremony starts early tomorrow."

"Yeah," said Megan. "Nighty-night."

"Sweet dreams," said Casey.

I put my head on the pillow and closed my eyes. "Good night, Intrepids. You're the best," I said.

And I meant it.

CHAPTER 18

THE awards ceremony was what my mom would call bittersweet. Everyone was happy and proud, receiving ribbons and trophies and hearing the applause, but there was a sad note underneath it all. In just a few short hours, we'd be saying our good-byes.

The visitors' day visitors, of course, were a very select group of family members—only Super relatives could attend, since the true purpose of the camp was a secret. Howie's visitor was his grandpa Gil.

I joined Howie in the mess hall just before he approached his grandpa.

"Just because you didn't get your powers this week doesn't mean they aren't on the way," I said.

"Actually," said Howie, "it kind of does."

"What do you mean?"

"Bertram and I had a long talk this morning," he said. "He

told me he's really proud of the way I captured the Sweep, and that I've been a great addition to Camp Courageous. But . . ."

I didn't like the sound of that *but*.

Howie sighed. "But he's seen thousands of superkids in his day and he's pretty certain that I'm not going to be one of them."

I felt a lump form in my throat. "Oh, Howie."

"Don't feel bad, Zoe," he said, smiling. "I had a great time here. No other ordinary kid in the world will ever get to see the stuff I saw. And I'm okay with not being super, honest. Frankly, I don't think I could handle it. The pressure must be nuts!"

"Well, there is that," I replied truthfully.

"Bertram had a great suggestion," Howie went on. "He thinks I could still be part of the superworld by becoming—get this— a dispatcher!"

My eyes lit up with excitement. "Like Thatcher!"

"Exactly," said Howie. "Of course, I won't have that whole rhyming-name thing happening. But Bertram says that dispatchers have to be able to think fast, and he said I've already proven that I'm great at that. And Thatcher and I have become pals over the last few days, so he's agreed to mentor me when the time comes."

"And when will that time be?" I asked, eager for Howie to get to do his part.

"Not for a while," he said. "I need to go to high school and college and maybe even graduate school first. But in the meantime, you can still talk to me about all your supermissions and stuff. Bertram said that would be perfectly okay, and I can even help you like I did here at camp."

"That's awesome!" I said, and I was so happy I hugged him.

Howie blushed. "Yeah."

My visitor, of course, was Grandpa Zack. And Zander's was his grandpa Zeb. I was able to spot Zeb easily—he looked a lot like my grandfather.

I wanted to go over and introduce myself, but Amanda was gathering the team together. We stood in a small circle around our counselor. For a moment, I was afraid she was going to tell us she was disappointed that we hadn't won.

"I just want to tell you how proud I am," she said, her eyes tearing up. "I couldn't have asked for a better bunch of superkids. I'll never forget you guys."

She hugged each of us. From the podium, Bertram was calling for quiet.

"Now we have two special presentations." He nodded at our little circle. "Will the Intrepid/Bravery team please come up here?"

We marched to the podium behind Amanda, wondering what was up.

"Your counselor Amanda has asked that you be given a special award in recognition of outstanding teamwork and quick thinking in the face of nearly insurmountable odds! So, to Team Intrepid/Bravery goes our first-ever Winning Isn't Everything Medal, created to remind us all that sometimes, true joy comes from simply being a part of something bigger than ourselves."

"Right!" said Amanda. "But next year . . . we're going to win!"

Everyone applauded as Bertram awarded us our medals, which were not gold or silver or even bronze. They were circles of yellow plastic cut out from our sunken raft! We all thought that was incredibly clever and way cool. In the background, I could hear Simon hammering his tiny fists on the glass door of the display cabinet. I saw Sam turn around and make the Loser sign at him once more, just for fun.

"Now," said Bertram, "I'll turn the podium over to Zander, who will make our second special surprise presentation."

When Zander stepped forward, I noticed the Fearless girls with their gold medals, sighing and giggling.

Grinning, Zander addressed the campers and their guests. "Today we're very lucky to have some special camp alumni visiting us. They've gone down in Camp Courageous history as the most magnificent team ever to play for the cup. Now, for the first time since they were our age, they're together again."

I glanced at my grandfather. Clearly, he'd had no idea this was coming. Neither had I.

"Will Zack, Zeb, and Gil please come up here," said Zander, "and take a bow!"

The kids erupted into cheers as the three heroes came forward. Bertram opened his arms and gave Zeb and then Gil giant bear hugs. Zeb and Gil shook hands.

Then Zeb and Zack turned to face each other.

I held my breath.

My grandfather gave Zeb a warm smile. "It's been a long time, cousin."

"Too long," said Zeb, returning the smile.

As the campers applauded and whistled, Zander caught my eye and we smiled, too. My grandfather was right. Family was the most important thing of all.

Saying good-bye to my teammates was one of the hardest things I've ever had to do. We hugged each other and cried a

136

little, and promised we'd IM and e-mail as often as we could. Melanie would be included, too, of course.

"I'm sure we'll end up being sent on supermissions together," I said.

"Yeah," said Casey. "And in the meantime, we can meet up to go shopping."

"Well, guys," said Megan, whose uncle Altitude was waiting for her, "I've gotta fly. . . ."

"Literally!" I said, and we all laughed.

Camp was over. It was time to go home.

On the ride home, Grandpa relayed what Zeb had told him.

"The thing was," he said, "that Zeb had always sort of looked up to me. He felt that I was the more advanced hero—although he was a darn powerful guy himself. And when his daughter, Zia, was super, he felt as though he was under a great deal of pressure to prove himself worthy of the responsibility. Which, of course, he was."

"It's funny," I said, remembering how Simon had worked so hard to make all of us doubt our own ability, "how even Supers like Simon can feel insecure about themselves. And I thought it was because he was stuck-up."

"Zeb was afraid I'd be angry or jealous that he was getting the chance to raise a superkid. I would have never felt that way, but he cared about me so much that he didn't want to take the chance of making me feel bad."

I shook my head. "I guess that's why he put so much pressure on Zander to be a winner, too. He needed to prove he could be a good mentor to a young Super."

"Well, we've worked it all out," said Grandpa. "So Zeb and I will be back in touch from here on in."

I heard a buzzing sound and reached into my backpack to answer my communication device.

"Kid Zoom," said Thatcher, "I've got Zander on wavelength Beta for you."

"Hi, Zander."

"Hi, Zoe. I just want to tell you that I had a long talk with my grandpa Zeb and he's going to go easier on me."

"That's great."

"I'm sure I'll always prefer winning to losing," he said, laughing, "but at least now, I'll be able to take it as it comes."

We made plans to get together with our grandfathers once school was under way and we were all back in the swing of our regular life—well, as regular as life ever got for secret superkids.

"I gotta hang up now," said Zander. "Thatcher's beeping in on the other wavelength."

"I bet it's one of those Fearless girls!" I joked.

"I hope so," said my cousin. "That redhead with the power to control the weather was kinda cute."

"Grandpa," I said as we drove down the shady country lane, "did you know that the Feds expect Zander and me to be the Super leaders of our generation?"

"Well," he said, grinning and giving me a sidelong glance, "I guess you could say I had a hunch."

I let that sink in. Talk about pressure. Still, I truly felt that Zander and I would be able to handle the responsibility.

"And what about Howie? Do you think his grandpa will ever get over the fact that he isn't going to be super?"

"I'm sure of it," said Grandpa Zack. "Howie may not have powers, but he is amazing in many other respects."

"True," I said. "Very, very true."

I leaned my head back against the car seat and closed my eyes. In a while, I'd get to see my mom and dad, and I was pretty sure there was already a lasagna in the oven, just waiting to be served for my homecoming dinner. And then I'd call Emily, and maybe tomorrow I'd see Josh Devlin, and soon I'd be getting ready to head back to school.

Back to the regular—fabulous—life of a secret superkid!